BARAKAH BEATS

Maleeha Siddiqui

SCHOLASTIC INC.

Copyright © 2021 by Maleeha Siddiqui

emojis © Shutterstock.com

This book was originally published in hardcover by Scholastic Press in 2021.

All rights reserved. Published by Scholastic Inc., *Publishers since 1920.* SCHOLASTIC and associated logos are trademarks and/or registered trademarks of Scholastic Inc.

The publisher does not have any control over and does not assume any responsibility for author or third-party websites or their content.

No part of this publication may be reproduced, stored in a retrieval system, or transmitted in any form or by any means, electronic, mechanical, photocopying, recording, or otherwise, without written permission of the publisher. For information regarding permission, write to Scholastic Inc., Attention: Permissions Department, 557 Broadway, New York, NY 10012.

This book is a work of fiction. Names, characters, places, and incidents are either the product of the author's imagination or are used fictitiously, and any resemblance to actual persons, living or dead, business establishments, events, or locales is entirely coincidental.

ISBN 978-1-338-70208-8

6 5 4 3 2   22 23 24 25 26

Printed in the U.S.A.   199

This edition first printing 2022

Book design by Yaffa Jaskoll

To my parents, for being the reason I stand on my own feet. To my husband, for never letting me quit my dreams. And to my daughter–this book is for you. I hope Mama made you proud.

1

Today's a big day for me—it's my Ameen. My family and I are celebrating me finishing my study of the Qur'an, and it looks like everyone in Northern Virginia was on the guest list. There are more than a hundred people in the banquet hall, all wearing nice suits or formal shalwar kameez. My best friend, Jenna Birdie, sticks out like a sore thumb with her white-blonde hair and periwinkle halter dress, especially next to me in my fancy green lehenga, which is basically a full-length embroidered skirt. But I'm glad she's here. I need the moral support.

"Just how many people did you invite?" Jenna whispers in my ear after the tenth person comes over to say salaam and hand me an envelope full of money. "They can't *all* be your family."

"No, just half of them," I say. Jenna's jaw drops.

When I finally have some space, I pick up the poofy skirt of my lehenga and we escape across the room to Mama and Baba, who are fiddling with the microphone onstage.

"Must be a big deal," Jenna says, looking around. "Reading the Qur'an, I mean."

I didn't just *read* the Qur'an. I memorized it by heart, making me a hafiza—someone who has completed the Hifz. And it *is* a big deal. That's why Mama and Baba wanted everyone to be here.

Jenna's leaving for a two-week tour of the UAE tomorrow, so she came *this close* to missing out. I'm glad she could make it. Jenna rarely gets to see the Pakistani Muslim side of my life even though we've been friends since we were four. We met at the park back when both of our moms stayed home. Jenna asked if I wanted to be a superhero with her. Together, we saved the park from certain doom, and that was that. We were friends for life. We had tons of playdates, and because we're neighbors, when Mrs. Birdie went back to work Jenna would always come over after school until one of her parents picked her up.

We used to talk about how we wished we went to the same school. Jenna has gone to public school her whole life, and I was homeschooled until I was eight. But then my parents enrolled me in Guided Light Academy's Hifz program, a private Islamic school, and we stopped talking about it. It's not like it affected my friendship with Jenna, anyway. I mean, come on. She gave me a Spider-Man sketchbook as a gift today. That's art and Tom Holland in one. You really can't know me better than that.

Onstage, Mama and Baba have to stop what they're doing to greet guests. Mama looks as uncomfortable as I feel in my heavy lehenga. She's not a fan of huge parties, and she's never been good at hiding it. I meet her eyes and she makes a silent choking face.

"Yes, Nimra graduated with top tajweed in her class," I overhear Baba say proudly to a man standing next to him. Baba's a hafiz, too. He doesn't mention that I ranked first out of only three girls, but I let him have his moment.

"Here, Mama." I give her the envelopes I collected.

"You're just going to hand over all that money?" Jenna squeals. "It's yours! You earned it!"

"No, honey," says Mama. "In Islam, kids pay the party bill." Judging by her reaction, I don't think Jenna gets the joke.

"Four years of hard work, Nimmy," Baba says, coming over to us. He hugs me to his side. "It paid off, didn't it?"

"Couldn't have done it without you," I say. "I'll never forget how you helped me get through Surah al-Baqarah." It's the longest and hardest chapter of the Qur'an to memorize. I would have given up without Baba's help.

"Nimra, please don't make him cry," says Mama. "He was getting emotional last night and this morning, too."

"I—I was not!" Baba sputters. "Well. Only a little."

"By the way, Reema and Hana can't make it," Mama says. "Reema's mom texted to tell me the kids are sick, and Hana's family ended up going to a funeral."

"Oh. Okay." Reema and Hana are the two other girls I did Hifz with. I feel bad that they aren't going to be here, but I'm a lot closer to Jenna than either of them. They're not my *best* friends. I'm kind of happy that I don't have to share my time with Jenna before she leaves. She's been busy with volleyball camp all summer and I barely get to see her anymore.

Nano appears at the stage with us. She's an older version of Mama, just slightly wrinklier, but I wouldn't tell her that. My grandmother loves when people think *I'm* her daughter.

"Maryam, what's taking so long?" she asks. "We need to get on with the program so the food can be served. It's rude to keep delaying."

"I'm still working on it, Mama," my mom says exasperatedly. "It hasn't been five minutes since the last time you asked." Mama's whole body tenses as she swats the microphone with her palm like it'll magically fix itself.

I pull on Nano's hand, refusing to let them argue. "Can we take pictures now?"

"Pehle yeh say karo," says Nano. She bends down to pull up my lehenga's waist until it feels like I have a wedgie and straightens my hijab. "There. Now let's go. Jenna can come, too."

I stand through picture after picture with my aunts, uncles, cousins, parents, and grandparents. It hurts to keep smiling, and I'm definitely going to have blisters on my feet. Just when I think it's never going to be over, Baba's voice booms through the speakers. "Testing one, two. Assalamu alaikum. Thank you, everyone, for coming out today to celebrate our daughter's great accomplishment. If I can please have you all take a seat. In shaa Allah, Nimra is going to say a few words and recite Surah Yasin for us."

"You're going to do what?" Jenna looks confused.

"I have to recite part of the Qur'an for our guests. It's tradition." Dread creeps over me. I'd rather take a hundred more pictures than go up there in front of everyone. "Wish me luck," I say, and with a deep breath, I plaster on a fake smile and head back to the stage alone. Baba passes me the mic with a reassuring nod.

Don't mess up, Nimra, don't mess up at your own Ameen. Everyone is watching.

I squeeze my eyes closed, wrap my hands tightly around the mic, and begin reciting Surah Yasin. It holds all the essential lessons of the Qur'an. I picked it out myself. Slowly, the familiar Arabic words flow easier and I'm brave enough to open my eyes again. As I stare out at the restaurant filled with people who have come out to support me, I feel something flutter inside my chest. This book brings all Muslims together and now I've got it word for word inside my head. I never thought about how cool that is.

Everyone claps when I'm done. I totally hear Baba sniffling behind me, but I know I nailed it when I spot Sister Sadia, my Hifz teacher, looking up at me onstage with shining eyes. I search the room for Jenna, eager to see what she thinks, and spot her sitting at a corner table by herself . . . looking down at her phone in her lap.

She wasn't even watching.

My stomach sinks, but I try not to let it hurt. Jenna's not Muslim, so I get why she's not *that* interested. My parents have always pushed me to make more Muslim friends. Not because they're better or anything, just, you know, *principle*. But what's the point in making other friends when I have Jenna? At least she's still here. So what if she doesn't get my faith? I don't understand why she likes sports, and they're a huge part of her life.

Now that the reading is over, the guests run toward the buffet like their chairs are on fire. It's their fault they're so hungry. Most of them showed up *one whole hour* after the time on the invitation.

"I'll make you a plate," Mama offers with her hands on my shoulders.

"First, I want to help you cut the cake," I say. Baba ordered my favorite—fresh vanilla cream and strawberry—with the words *Congratulations, Hafiza Nimra!* written on top in green icing. I want a big piece of cake more than the biryani being served. It's not Nano's biryani, so it's not going to taste as good anyway.

Jenna comes over to help, too. She and I hand Mama and Nano plates and spoons as they cut up pieces of cake. I start making a rainbow pattern on the table with the napkins and Jenna copies me. She sticks her finger in one slice and licks off the frosting. Then she tries to sneak-attack a glob on my nose. I make giggle-gagging noises while fending her off.

It's only then that I hear what Mama and Nano are talking about.

"Did you see that article I sent you?" says Nano. "See how hot your field is right now? Companies are practically begging for people! Why did you go to college if you weren't going to use your degree?"

"I really don't think this is the place to talk about it," Mama whispers.

"Maryam, you have wasted so much of your life already. This business you two are starting is not as stable as a real job."

Mama and Nano glare at each other. They're not even talking in Urdu. Jenna can understand every word. It's like we're invisible.

"Besides," Nano continues, "Nimra doesn't need you to look after her anymore. She's *twelve*. When she starts going to a real school, she'll catch up with all the other kids on her own."

My eyes widen at hearing that. Does Nano think less of me because I go to Islamic school? But I just memorized the whole Qur'an! Girls rarely do that because most people think it's useless. Girls don't lead namaz or taraweeh prayer during Ramadan like boys do, either, but that only made me want to do Hifz more. I wanted to stand out. Be special.

I don't feel very special right now.

"Nimra will always need me, Mama, because I'm her *mother*," Mama fires back. "And as for my career, I will do what I think is best for me and my family. I don't care log kya kahenge."

What will people say? Mama rebels against that phrase all the time. Signing me up for Hifz was one way. Quitting her day job to raise me was another. My parents and grandparents don't often see eye to eye, and there've been a lot of fights since I was little about this "bad" choice or that "wrong" decision. Nano and Nana always want the opposite of what Mama and Baba want. My mom says it's because she grew up in America, while her parents grew up in Pakistan. They raised Mama with a lot of cultural things she wants to change because they don't align with Islam's teachings. Mama thinks it's wrong that some people still follow culture over religion when Islam makes life easier in so many ways.

"You think you know everything," Nano snaps. "For once, maybe you should consider that what other people are trying to tell you is for your own good."

Baba arrives with a full plate. "Who's hungry?"

One look at Mama and Nano tells him what he just walked into, and his smile disappears in a wink. "Nimra, why don't you and Jenna go get food and sit down?" he asks. "I'll take over here."

Jenna's more than happy to escape the awkward situation. I almost drop a plate as she drags me away by the elbow.

"Phew. That was close," Jenna says, mock wiping sweat from her forehead.

"They always do this," I huff under my breath. "They never stop. Not even today. Adults ruin everything."

Jenna puts her arm around my shoulders. "Hey, come on. It's your big day. Cheer up!"

But I'm too busy watching my parents and grandmother argue quietly near the cake, which I don't even want anymore. I wish I had my sketch pad and pencil right now. I'd find some peace and quiet and forget all about them fighting.

"How come you never tell them to stop?" Jenna asks.

"What's the point?" I say quietly. "They won't listen."

I love both my parents and grandparents a ton, but I can't stand them when they're in the same room together. They're like Thor and Loki. Deep down they care about one another, but they're a pain in the neck most of the time. It hurts the most when they fight about me, which happens a *lot*. I tell myself not to butt in. Not like I can anyway; I always freeze up. So instead, I take it all out on paper. I've drawn some pretty good pictures while I cried.

"Nimraaaaa," Jenna says, lightly shaking me. "Don't be upset. I got your back." She holds up her fists like she's ready to punch somebody. I crack a tiny smile despite myself, which is something no one else can make me do at times like this.

"Hey, what if I ask my parents if I can sleep over at your place tonight?" Jenna asks. "I don't have to wake up early because our flight's not till tomorrow night. We can watch *Infinity War!*" Jenna and I have watched the Avengers movies at least a hundred times. They never get as old as my family's craziness. Jenna pokes my face in a teasing gesture. "I know you can't say no to Tom Holland."

She's right. I can't.

I sigh, finally grinning wider. "Yeah, I'd like that."

"Duh you would. Now come on. I'm starving. Race you to the buffet!" Jenna laughs like an evil villain and takes off before I can even lift up my lehenga.

I gather up my skirts and chase after her.

2

I bawl my eyes out when the credits start rolling on the wall-mounted TV. Beside me, Jenna lies flat on her stomach with her legs crossed in the air. She throws a pillow at my face, smiling. "Seriously, Nimra. Every time? It's just a movie, you loser."

"Take that back!" I laugh. "You know I can't help it."

We're in my basement in our pajamas with blankets scattered all around us. My parents converted the space into an in-law suite for when my dadi and dada come to visit or if other relatives stay over. But when it's empty, I pretend like it's my own apartment and that I live someplace cool and artsy by myself. There's a bedroom, comfy couches, a TV, and even a small kitchenette with a pantry filled with snacks.

I pause the credits and run my hands across the new sketchbook that sits open in my lap, mostly out of habit. The weight is comforting. I chew on the end of one of my side braids and look over at Jenna. She's flipping through pictures on her phone. Over her shoulder, I see her tap a group shot of herself huddled with other girls in black spandex. She attaches it to a text and sends it. I look down at my blank page before she notices me snooping.

Jenna turns over onto her side to look at me. Her hair slides out of its sloppy bun. "So, when are your parents going to buy you a phone?"

"They don't think I need one," I say, shrugging. "I don't really think I do either."

"You're so missing out. How are you going to see all my Dubai photos?" Jenna pouts. "I need your likes."

"You could show them to me when you get back."

Jenna stares at me like that's the most absurd thing she's ever heard. "You sound like Val. She's barely on. You're both nuts."

I sit up. "Who's Val?"

"Valentina. The one from school. You met her at my birthday party last year."

"The one you had at the bowling alley?" I nudge her side with my bare foot. "Jenna, I wasn't there. We were in Canada that weekend."

"Really?" Jenna flops onto her back next to me. "Huh. Guess I forgot."

I frown. How does she not remember that? I'm about to pick on her for it when Mama and Baba walk in.

"Hey, girls. You doing fine?" asks Mama. "Did you have fun at the party, Jenna?"

Jenna gives her a thumbs-up. "Yeah, Mrs. Sharif. Five stars. But you know what would've made it even more fun?" She pauses for dramatic effect. "Dancing! It was a party! How come there wasn't any music? Me and Nimra would've torn up the dance floor."

I glance at Mama and Baba, wondering what they'll tell her. They've taught me my whole life that Islam doesn't allow musical instruments. Of course, Muslims around the world have different interpretations. It's a huge controversy. Some think that music is only wrong if it contains dirty lyrics or goes against Islam's teachings.

Others avoid it altogether. My parents and I listen to music, so it's not like I have to be sneaky about it, but we have strict boundaries. None of us play an instrument or go to concerts or dance at parties and stuff. And we don't think that we're better than people who do. That's even more wrong. Only Allah has the right to judge us. But it's still really hard to explain that to people who won't get it. I realize it's never come up with Jenna before.

"It was a celebration of Nimra completing Hifz," Mama says. "It wouldn't have been appropriate. Besides, it's not something that our family generally does."

"Oh." Jenna's wearing the same expression as the time I told her we can't even drink water when we're fasting for Ramadan. I think the athlete inside her died that day.

I change the subject. Jenna's my best friend, but I don't like talking about religion with her. Plus, I'm curious to know why Mama and Baba came to check in on us when they should already be in bed. "Did you guys need something?" I ask my parents.

"Yes, actually. We were wondering if we could have a minute. There's something we want to talk to Nimra about," says Mama.

Jenna starts climbing to her feet. "Should I leave?"

"No, Jenna. You can stay," Baba says. "In fact, it's probably better if you do." My parents sit themselves on the sofa like they're in a business meeting. One in which everyone's wearing their nightie. I fidget with my sketchbook's spiral. What exactly are they doing?

Mama and Baba exchange a glance and it feels like an eternity before Mama says, "What do you think about switching over to Farmwell for seventh grade?"

"You want me to go to *public* school?" I squeak. "Now? I thought I wasn't going until high school!"

"We know it's kind of sudden, but after talking about it, we think it's a good time for you to move over," Baba says. "The plan was for you to finish through the eighth grade at GLA, but that was only to give you enough time to complete Hifz. You finished a lot faster than we anticipated, and it sort of caught us by surprise. Sister Sadia said you practically flew through the last couple of juz'."

"How about it, Nimmy?" Mama asks. "There's nothing wrong with starting early. Plus, you two will finally get to go to the same school just like you always wanted."

I lose track of all time for a minute. I was not prepared for this, but what they're saying makes sense. I didn't think about it before because I was too busy focusing on completing my memorization. But now that the news is sinking in, excitement streaks through me like a comet. Me. In public school. I can take my first official art class, something I didn't think I'd be able to do until I was a freshman. *And Jenna will be there, too!* A huge grin splits my face at the thought of seeing my best friend every day. It's basically our dream come true.

I round on Jenna to give her an excited hug. It's the best idea ever! Jenna looks at me, then slowly lifts one shoulder, like, *Yay?*

I frown, my enthusiasm popping like a bubble. My parents are suggesting I go to public school for the first time, and all Jenna can do is *shrug?*

My confused silence must've stretched too long because Mama says, "We thought you'd be more thrilled."

I am, but I don't want to be the *only* one who feels that way. I think of a lousy excuse to distract Mama. "Well, I don't know how to go to public school."

"Don't worry, beta. We know you can do it. Besides, you already have a professional at your side."

Jenna flips her hair when Mama's gaze lands on her. "That's me. The professional. At your service." There's something weird about Jenna's reaction that I can't quite read.

"See? You'll adjust in no time," Baba says. "We think this is the best thing for you, Nimmy. Trust us."

Something's telling me I don't have a choice except to listen to Mama and Baba. They're obviously just being nice by pretending to ask for my opinion.

"Okay, fine," I say. My parents clap like I just said my first word and start talking at the same time about how I'm going to love it, I'm going to fit right in, it's a new opportunity, blah blah BLAH. All things parents say to convince themselves they aren't wrong. Meanwhile, Jenna finally perks up, but it's not for the reason that I was hoping for.

"Wait, does this mean Nimra finally gets a phone?" she asks.

3

According to Google and Netflix, in public school it's okay to wear sweatpants or leggings every day. There's gross cafeteria food, smelly gyms, classrooms full of twenty-odd children going through puberty, and *no recess*. Urban Dictionary calls middle school the fifth circle of hell. Some guy called Dante wrote a poem all about it.

My eyes rake over my new iPhone's screen, then back to my gutted closet. I don't have anything to wear for my first day in hell. At least, I don't own anything like the pictures of acceptable outfits Jenna texted me this morning with a helpful tip: NO SPARKLES OR BUTT BRANDING! THEY'RE DEAD.

"Mama!" I yell.

Footsteps sound up the stairs and my mom comes rushing into my room. "What happened?" She's still in her pajamas and her hair is in its usual topknot. I can only dream of looking as cute in the morning. People are always saying that Mama got "good" genes. She insists it's because she had me at a young age compared with her friends, but I always catch her smiling to herself later.

"I'm having a crisis. Help me!"

"You're still deciding?" Mama asks, taking in the mess. "You've been at it since Fajr! Nimmy, you have plenty of clothes." Mama crosses her arms in that adult way that says she thinks I'm being ridiculous. "Just pick something. You're going to school, not a fashion show."

Easy for her to say. She and Baba both work from home all day. They're not the ones suddenly being thrown into the seventh grade after years in Islamic school. I'm beginning to think this whole public-school thing is the wrong move because, man, this is so much stress. I blew through almost half of the pages in my new sketchbook in the last two weeks.

At least I have Jenna. She's walking me to school and promised to show me around. I'm sure it won't be so bad once I figure this whole wardrobe thing out. Still, now that I see her outfit pictures, I realize I should've had Mama take me shopping. If only Jenna had sent them over sooner. I'm too used to wearing a plain black abaya to class every day.

I hold my phone out to Mama. "I need something cool like this."

Mama crinkles her nose at the pictures. "You're not Jenna, Nimra. You don't have to dress like that. Jeans and a T-shirt will be just fine." She hands them to me from the pile of clothes on the floor. "Here. Hurry up, or your halwa will turn cold."

My eyes light up. "Halwa? Did Nano make it?" My grandmother makes the best food. Mama doesn't like cooking, so Baba does most of it, but his halwa can't touch Nano's. Most food doesn't even come close.

"She dropped it off last night while you were sleeping, along with a gift. Be quick or Baba will eat your share."

Not on my watch, I think, and make a beeline for the bathroom. I wash my face, brush my teeth, and throw a cardigan on over my short-sleeved shirt even though it's already eighty degrees out. I'm so close to pinning my favorite navy-blue hijab on in front of the mirror when I remember Jenna's no-sparkles warning. Surely I can get away with a few twinkling stars on my headscarf.

I finish pinning my hijab, then skip down the stairs in record time. I'm so fixated on catching up to the smell of delicious halwa that I almost run right into a tower of cardboard boxes stacked in the middle of our living room. Then I *actually* fall backward over an open case of multi-vitamins. Baba pokes his head around the wall just in time to see me land on my butt. He bursts out laughing.

"Not funny," I grumble, massaging my rear end.

Mama and Baba's online over-the-counter generics business has been swallowing up every square inch of our little town house. There's stuff everywhere, bubble wrap and packing paper crowding the sofas, even more boxes on top of our dining table. Bottles of pain relievers, omega-3 fish oil soft gels, and nutrients for hair loss. When Mama quit her biotech job, she and Baba set out to realize their dream of being business owners. Even Baba left his old engineering position a few months ago to help expand the business (spoiler alert: It's growing fast).

"When are you guys getting that warehouse?" I ask. "There's barely any room to walk in here."

"Soon, in shaa Allah," Mama promises. "We were just talking about it. We need to hire employees, too. Can't run everything on our own anymore." She sets a heaping bowl of halwa with freshly made puri on the counter. I practically drool at the sight.

"You said Nano brought me a present?" I ask through a mouthful of the carroty sweet. Mama hands me a small gift bag from behind the counter and I eagerly tear open the tissue wrap to find a new notebook, a bag of Jolly Ranchers, and twenty dollars inside a card that reads *Good luck on your first day of school!*

"Don't forget to call and say thank you," says Mama.

"Right. I can text her now." Maybe it's because I'm still getting used to it, but I don't see what the big deal is about owning a cell phone. It's just a mini tablet. The screen's not even big enough to draw on.

"Well, Maryam, the day's finally come," Baba tells Mama gravely. "Our daughter's joined the dark side. We protected her for as long as we could, but she's technology's slave now." He shakes his head and goes back to playing Diner Dash on his tablet.

I roll my eyes as I shoot off a thank-you message to Nano with a trillion emojis, then go back to eating. Only after noticing that my chewing sounds too loud even to my own ears do I look up to find both my parents peering at me. "What?" I blurt. "Do I have something on my face?"

"Tell us how you're really feeling, Nimra," Mama says, leaning forward on the counter. "Are you nervous? Scared? I went to public school my whole life, you know. I think it can be way more fun." My mom is trying to sound convincing, like that one time I came down with diarrhea on a trip to Pakistan and she told me Pepto-Bismol tasted like bubble gum to get me to take it. I haven't looked at bubble gum the same way since.

"It's normal to feel nervous," says Baba. "But just remember what I always say."

"If it's not broken, take it apart and fix it?" I ask.

"Well, yeah . . . and now you know why I'm not a doctor," Baba says. "I mean, no. The *other* thing that I always say." He puts his hand on top of my head. "'Just be yourself.' This is a new beginning for you. A clean slate. You can do anything if you put your mind to it."

Mama and I exchange a look at his dorkiness, but a smile creeps up my lips anyway. Baba's wisdom always has a way of making me feel better. It reminds me of something else, too. "So, if I can do anything, why can't I take art instead of Spanish?" I ask sweetly.

Mama and Baba insisted that I take a language, but that meant I didn't have any room left in my schedule to take art. I've been fighting them about it for two weeks, but they won't let it go. It's probably too late to change anything, but that doesn't mean I'm not going to keep trying to change their minds.

"We've been over this," Mama says. "You already know how to draw. Learning other languages opens up a lot of doors for you in the real world."

"But art is important, too! And it's not just about drawing."

Mama gives me a stern look from across the counter. "End of discussion, Nimra."

I shove my bowl away, preparing to take another stab at convincing them, but then the doorbell rings. "That's Jenna!"

I hop off the stool and run to the door. I throw it open

and my jaw drops. Jenna looks like she walked straight out of a commercial, makeup and all. She's tan, too. I look down at my boring outfit and sigh. I knew jeans and a T-shirt weren't going to cut it.

"Hey!" Jenna gives me a hug. Her shiny blonde pony-tail tickles my face. "OMG, I can't believe we're finally going to the same school together! It's going to be so weird seeing you in the hallways. In a good way." Jenna follows me to the kitchen, dodging the vitamin chaos at the front of our house. "Hi, Mr. and Mrs. Sharif!"

"Hey, Jenna. How was your trip?" Mama asks.

"It was awesome!" Jenna replies. "We went skiing in the Mall of the Emirates and went up the Burj Khalifa at night. And I rode a camel in the desert!" Jenna fans her face. "But it was *so* hot! I thought I was going to melt."

"Well, we're glad you made it back in solid state," Baba says, and winks at me over Jenna's shoulder. I giggle.

Jenna bumps my shoulder. "Ready?"

I nod, grateful that our school is close enough so we can walk. Jenna told me if middle school's the fifth circle of hell, then school buses are the fourth circle.

Mama hands me my lunch box. Baba kisses my

forehead. "Have a great day, kiddo. We can't wait to hear all about it. Allah hafiz."

"Wait," Jenna says as I sling my bag over my shoulders. "Nimra, you forgot your scarf."

"No, I didn't, silly. It's right here." I point at my snugly wrapped head.

Jenna frowns, blue eyes confused. "I meant you forgot to take it off." Her smile droops. "Wait. Are you going to school with it on?"

Mama and Baba stop in the middle of their conversation about a customer's email to look over at Jenna.

My face grows hot. "Yeeaaahhh," I say slowly. "Why is that a surprise? I wear it everywhere."

"Oh, I thought . . . you wouldn't have to for public school," says Jenna. She looks like she wants to say more, but her mouth forms a tight line instead.

What on earth gave her that idea?

Baba starts to get up from the table. "Want me to walk with you, Nimmy?"

I hold up my hands. "No!" Even I know having your parents walk you to your first day of seventh grade is social suicide. And no one in a hundred-mile radius of Farmwell

Station Middle School is ever going to hear my dad call me Nimmy. "It's fine, Baba. We're gonna go now. Bye!"

I drag Jenna out the door before my parents can protest, but their concerned faces follow me all the way through the park, over the rickety old bridge in the woods, and across the blacktop to school.

4

When we get to Farmwell, Jenna takes me to the front office to meet Principal Coggins. She's a kind-looking lady in a fancy suit, loud heels, and dark lipstick. I shake her hand and she clasps both of mine with a fierce sort of energy.

"Welcome to the Falcon family, Nimra!" Principal Coggins chimes. "We're so happy to have you here. If there's absolutely anything we can do to make your first day a success, please don't hesitate to ask. My door is always open. Unless I'm in a meeting. Or at lunch. Or I quit."

Principal Coggins cackles like it's the funniest thing

ever. Jenna and I bite our lips to keep from cracking up. Somehow, I don't think she's kidding about that last one. Grown-ups like to hide their true feelings behind cheesy jokes and sarcasm a lot more than kids. It probably has something to do with getting older.

"Jenna's going to give you the grand tour and drop you off at homeroom. Have you had a chance to look over your schedule?" Principal Coggins asks. I nod yes, even though the guidance counselor's instructions made as much sense as chicken fingers. Chickens don't have fingers.

Principal Coggins takes out two slips of paper, signing them with a bright pink pen before handing them to Jenna and me. "Take your time. Don't worry about being late to class. I know this is a much bigger building than what you're used to, but it's very easy to navigate once you get the hang of it. I hope to see you around."

"She seems nice," I say to Jenna as we leave the main office.

"She needs to cut back on the coffee." Jenna takes my hand and speeds up. "Let's go to your locker first."

The school's laid out in three sections, one appointed

to each grade: House A for eighth, House B for seventh, and House C for sixth. In House B, Jenna teaches me how to open my locker, and after four tries I finally get it.

"Where is everybody?" I ask, looking around at the empty corridors. It's not like we're early.

"Oh, we can't hang out in the hallways before school anymore. There was an incident a few years back in House A, and now each grade has to be supervised." Jenna ticks them off on her manicured fingers. "Sixth grade gets the main gym; seventh grade, cafeteria; eighth grade, auditorium. Do you have your schedule?" I give it to her, watching her face as she goes over it. "Hey, we have PE together on B days! Algebra I?" she snorts. "You nerd. I bet you'll be the only seventh grader in that class. Oh. You have Myer for social studies. I hear he's tough and kinda harsh." I gulp, imagining the devil-smile purple-horned emoji. "All right. Let's start in the main gym."

She shows me both gyms, one of which is packed with high-strung sixth graders. I already know I'm going to hate PE. I don't have an active bone in my body. We didn't have to do any sort of physical activity at my old school. Reema, Hana, and I would shoot hoops on the basketball court during breaks sometimes, or Sister Sadia would take us out to the field to kick a soccer ball around if the weather was nice.

"We have eight classes total," Jenna explains as we cut past the library. "Our schedules are broken up into two different days, A days and B days, with four blocks each day. Blocks one through four are on A days, and five through eight are on B days. Lunch is during blocks three and seven and also has four different times: A, B, C, and D. You have five minutes to get to class between blocks. Make sense so far?"

I nod, even though I'm overwhelmed. I have to jog to keep up with Jenna's longer strides. Five minutes! In this maze? Every single hallway looks exactly the same. I'm going to look like a complete newbie trying to find my way around. I already miss being in one classroom with the same teacher all day.

After Jenna shows me the cafeteria, auditorium, nurse's office, and where all my classes are, she steers me toward my homeroom. "And that's it! Pretty easy, right?" she asks.

I slouch against the turquoise-and-maroon-patterned wall. I've never wanted so badly to just lock myself up in my room with a sketch pad until my hands are covered in lead. "Is it time to go home yet?"

"Oh, you'll be fine," Jenna says. "You'll be an expert in no time. Know how Peter Parker totally sucked at the whole Spider-Man thing before Tony Stark whipped him into shape?" Jenna puts her arm around my shoulder and squeezes. "I'm your Mr. Stark. And I'm here to tell you, you got this, kid." Her faith in me raises my spirits just a smidge. If she thinks I can do this whole middle school thing, then maybe I can.

"Is there a fancy high-tech suit in it for me?" I ask.

"Sorry. I used up all my allowance on a new curling iron. Besides, you're the *artiste*. Draw one yourself. Anyway, I gotta go." Jenna hustles backward down the hall, waving. "I have to give something back to a friend. Text me if you get lost!" I raise my hand halfway, but she's already gone.

The bell rings, making me jump. The halls start filling up and students file past me to take their seats. A few people give me curious glances. I snap out of it and join them, startling when I realize where I am. My homeroom is in an art classroom! A giant color wheel poster is taped to the front board, and long tables sit in a rectangle around the room in front of paint-crusted sinks. I take everything in wistfully. It feels like I brought a piece of home here with me.

I sit down at the front of the room, relaxing just a little, until a girl comes up to me. She has straight black hair and deeply tanned skin. Her teeth flash pearl white when she gives me a smile. "Hi. You. Must. Be. Jenna's. Neighbor. I'm. Julie. It's. Nice. To. Meet. You."

Why is she talking like that? Then it hits me, and my face turns red. "I can speak English," I say a little too loudly. Heads turn in our direction in surprise.

Julie's mouth hangs in embarrassment. "Oh, sorry! I didn't—my bad. Jenna said you came from a small religious school."

"Yeah, so? I was born here in Virginia." I'm using the same tone as Mama when she accuses Nano of being hypocritical or sexist or racist. You can find all kinds of people in Northern Virginia: Black, white, and brown. Muslims aren't exactly that hard to find, and some of us have been in America for a really long time. We even speak English at home. I only talk in Urdu to my dad's family in Pakistan, even though it's kind of broken and they make fun of my American accent.

Wait a second. How does Julie think I've been talking to Jenna for eight years? Unless Jenna hadn't told her about me until recently. The thought brings a bad taste to my mouth.

Before I can say anything else, our homeroom teacher, Ms. Scott, calls for attention and Julie scuttles away. We sit through morning announcements welcoming everyone back from summer vacation, but I can't hear anything over all the other students chattering about break and comparing schedules and making funny faces at Principal Coggins's voice over the intercom.

Ms. Scott passes out agendas for the new school year and the bell rings again. I've already forgotten the way to my first block when it's time to go, but everyone's moving too fast for me to stop them and ask for directions. A couple of South Asian kids in the hallway catch my eye but quickly look away. Nobody stops at my look of helplessness. As far as I can tell, I'm the only one wearing hijab.

I don't get it. If I saw someone I thought was new, I would try and help them right away.

I barely make it to social studies on time and have to sprint before the teacher shuts the door in my face.

"Cutting it close there," Mr. Myer says, shrewd eyes squinting at me from behind his glasses. "Let's not make it a habit. I'd like to write fewer lunch detention slips this year."

"I'm new," I explain. "This is my first time in public school."

"Well, from here on out it won't be your first time, will it? You'll be a seasoned public-school goer."

Sheesh, who spat in his coffee this morning? Why be a teacher if you're just going to hate on kids? Sister Sadia was always so sweet. She had the kind of smile that felt like a hug. Mr. Myer looks like he'd rather get poked in the eyes than be in a room full of seventh graders.

Being almost tardy leaves me one empty chair in the back of the class next to a Black girl who smiles shyly at me as I sit down. She looks more like nine than twelve, with hair in a twisted up-bun. She doesn't say anything, just opens her glittery purple binder to start putting in the printed notes Mr. Myer hands out. I start organizing mine, too, when a thick packet of paper slaps down in front of me. Puzzled, I look up to see Mr. Myer standing over me.

"This is a review packet of everything that's taught in sixth-grade social studies," says Mr. Myer. He gives me a snobby look over his square glasses. "Studying it will help you catch up with the rest of the class. I don't have time to help students who fall behind."

My face turns red as a stoplight. My parents were worried the school would make a huge fuss about my records, but it turns out I'm already caught up with everything they've been doing in public school. I'm even in a higher-level math class. "I don't need it. I already learned this stuff last year."

"We'll see. I think you'll find that our curriculum is more challenging compared with what you're used to." Mr. Myer smiles like I'm a bug he can't wait to squash and moves on.

I'm so shocked I can't even respond. I put my hands underneath my desk to hide their shaking. The quiet girl shoots me an apologetic look, but it doesn't make me feel better.

I take the review packet and stuff it into my backpack to throw away after class.

The day doesn't get much better after that. In every class, I have to tell people how to pronounce my name right. I've been called *Neem*ra instead of *Nim*ra three times already. I give up correcting people after the fourth time.

By third block, I just want lunch to hurry up so I can find Jenna and tell her about my day. But my Algebra I class is in D lunch, which means I have to wait until the very end of class to see her, and that is *if* we have the same lunch period. The thought of having to eat with the older kids gives me a stomachache. Jenna was right: I can tell that I'm the only seventh grader in algebra because I started recognizing a few faces in my other classes, and this one's got none of them.

Ms. Yariks announces a pop quiz on the material we were supposed to learn over the summer, and everyone starts to complain.

"That's not fair!" one of the girls whines. "We just got back! I have vacation brain."

"Oh, just you wait until high school," Ms. Yariks says in a thick Southern accent. "You'll come running back here asking for a pop quiz from me every day."

Urban Dictionary called high school the ninth circle of hell. Great. Something to look forward to if I survive out here first.

Ms. Yariks sits at her desk while we quietly take the quiz. It's basic pre-algebra review. So easy. I fly through the first five questions, then stop to chew on my pencil's eraser, trying to solve number six. I'm still chewing when someone nudges my left elbow. Must be a mistake.

But then it happens again. "Psst." What in the world? I sneak a peek at the brown boy next to me. He's looking down at his paper, and I think I might be hearing things when he whispers, "You did number five wrong."

I look up to make sure Ms. Yariks didn't see. Luckily, she's busy on her phone and missed the boy's obvious attempt at cheating. But now I'm annoyed because there's *no way* that I—

Rats! I forgot to simplify my equation! He's right. I erase my answer, write in the correct one, and move on. I guess I should thank the boy, but I'm afraid of looking suspicious. I try to get his attention after we hand in our quizzes, but he turns his back to me to talk to a friend and doesn't acknowledge me again for the rest of class. The whole time, I get this weird nagging feeling like I know him from somewhere.

Or maybe it's just happiness from someone finally showing me a little kindness today. Even if it was dishonest.

5

Our class files out for lunch and I scan the cafeteria for Jenna. I'm filled with relief when I find her sitting at one of the long tables with other girls in our grade in what looks like their usual spot. Clutching my lunch box, I go over and poke her in the shoulder with a huge smile on my face.

Jenna looks surprised to see me there. "Oh, hey, Nimra. You're in this lunch, too?"

"Yup. I just got out of algebra. Scooch?"

Jenna hesitates for a second, then makes room for me on the bench. She introduces me to the girls sitting closest to us. "It sounds like you've already met Julie." Julie nods, but doesn't smile or say anything. Jenna waves her hand to a brown-haired Latina girl at the table. "This is Val Lopez. And that's Evelyn Carr."

"We have social studies together," Evelyn says to me, tying her golden-blonde hair back with a ribbon. "I told them how Mr. Myer was a big jerk to you."

They were talking about me? I look over at Julie. She probably thinks I deserved it. I was a *little* harsh in homeroom.

"So, how's your first day been?" Jenna asks. Her butt's almost hanging off the bench from the way she's sitting so that she's facing the other girls more than she's facing me. I wish we were eating alone so that I could be more open with her. I'm not used to having other kids around when I'm with Jenna. It's always just been the two of us wher-ever we went—the movies, the mall, and even the Afghan restaurant we go to for my birthday every year. Mama and Baba always take me and Jenna for cheesecake afterward.

I unwrap my sandwich, suddenly not hungry. I'm not even excited about eating the peanut butter Oreos Mama packed. "It's okay. Different."

"How big was your old school?" Evelyn asks, loudly breaking a pretzel between her teeth.

"Well, the boys and girls were separate. There were way more boys. But in my class, there were three girls including me."

"Only *three*?" Val cries. "This place must seem giant to you! I can't imagine going to school with the same three people every day. Didn't you get bored?"

I shrug. "I was used to it." But they've already moved on. Evelyn brings up the topic of volleyball with Jenna. They're on the same youth team. Julie plays softball and Val is a cheerleader. The more they talk, the further I get pushed out of the circle—if I was even in it to begin with. Jenna's not making any effort to include me, but it's probably because she knows I understand sports about as well as I get astrophysics. At one point, Jenna looks over at me when the other three are talking and smiles. She offers me her bag of chips, but when I decline, she just shrugs and goes back to listening to her friends' conversation instead of striking one up with me.

I feel off about what's happening here, but I'm having trouble putting it into words. Between school and sports, I've always known Jenna had other friends. She's told me stories before, but I always thought *I* was her best friend. Jenna has every right to hang out with whoever she wants, but watching her goof off with Evelyn, Val, and Julie feels like taking a knee to my chest.

Val notices me sitting there quietly and turns to me. "Do you play any sports, Nimra?"

"No, I draw." I want to slap my forehead. Wow. Talk about wrong answer.

Val scrunches her eyebrows. "You draw? Like pictures?" *What else?* "You're an artist?"

"No, Nimra can't be an artist," Julie butts in icily. "My mom's an artist. A *real* artist. She sells her paintings online and everything. Doodling for fun doesn't count." The lunchroom suddenly feels like someone's cranked up the heat. I can't even find my voice.

Evelyn changes the subject back to athletics. "You wouldn't be able to do sports in that thing anyway, right? Wouldn't you get super-duper hot and sweaty?"

That *thing?* "Ibtihaj Muhammad is an Olympic athlete who wears hijab," I say in as normal a voice as I can. "I just don't like sports."

A scream bounces off the cafeteria walls and everyone swings their head to stare at a group of eighth-grade boys sitting right behind our table. One of them has sticky, carbonized fizz all over his face. A teacher marches over there to scold them. My attention snags on a boy in a red polo laughing at the friend who got pranked. It's him, the one who helped me on my algebra quiz.

"Hey." I pull on Jenna's sleeve. "Who's that?"

She follows my pointing finger and, like, *giggles*. "Who, Waleed? Why? Do you think he's cute?"

I'm horrified. "No. Just curious." I know that doesn't help, but I still can't shake the sense I know him from somewhere.

"Suuuure," Jenna drawls. "Don't get any ideas. He's an eighth grader. And a super-popular one, too. He and his best friends, Matthew"—Jenna gestures toward the white, sandy-haired boy drenched in soda—"and Bilal"—she points to a Black kid in a green shirt—"are in a band."

"And they're *really* good," Evelyn gushes. "You should check out their SoundCloud, if you're into hip-hop or rap. The entire school is obsessed."

Just like that, it strikes me. "Wait, I do know him! Waleed's dad leads taraweeh every year at the masjid. I see him around sometimes, too."

"The what?" asks Julie.

"Oh, crap!" The word *masjid* reminds me that it's time for Zuhr—the noon prayer. My eyes fly to the clock. Lunch is the only time I have to pray at school, and I forgot to ask about a room before school started like my parents told me to. I pack up what's left of my lunch and spring to my feet. "I have to go! I'll see you later."

Principal Coggins is standing in the middle of the lunchroom watching all the students like a hawk. "Nimra!" she greets me when I go up to her. "What can I do for you?"

"I need a place to pray. Someplace clean and quiet," I tell her.

Principal Coggins pauses, pursing her dark lips thoughtfully. "Oh. Well, I don't know—"

"Band room." The quiet voice comes from a table behind Principal Coggins, where the shy girl from my social studies class is eating lunch alone with a book open in front of her. "There's a small room next to the bigger band room that's empty during this block. The band teachers said it's okay to use. I prayed before coming here."

"There you go!" Principal Coggins says. "Thank you, Khadijah. Nimra, the band room is right across from the auditorium."

Khadijah. And she prays, too! But I don't have time to dwell on it. Lunch is almost over. I dash to the bathroom to make wudu—the ritual cleansing. I make it fast because I don't want anyone to walk in and see me with my feet in the sink.

The room Khadijah told me about is small but not too stuffy. It's windowless, but there are a couple of chairs and a podium with a whiteboard on the wall behind it. Someone wrote out a music scale in blue marker for what looks like a lesson from earlier in the day. I move everything out of the way and shut the door. I don't have a prayer rug with me, but at least the white tile floor looks clean. Using the compass app Baba downloaded for me on my phone, I locate the direction of the qibla and face it.

I relax, releasing all my stress just as Sister Sadia taught me to. Up, recite, down, recite, kneel, recite. I'm usually good at staying focused, but Jenna's weirdness in the cafeteria keeps distracting me. Up, recite, down, recite, kneel, recite. Is she back to acting all nice with her friends now that I'm gone? Could I have possibly imagined it? What if—?

In the middle of my third rak'a comes a BANG that scares me half to death.

My eyes fly open, my heart thudding loudly in my chest. WHAT THE HECK?

"Jeez, Matthew, watch where you're going!"

"It wasn't my fault! Somebody left it right in front of the door."

The voices were coming from the other band room. Annoyed, I gather myself and start the next round, trying to concentrate over the noise traveling across the tiny hallway into my little sanctuary, when a symphony of drums, guitar, and singing strikes up next door. You have got to be kidding me!

I want so badly to go over there and tell whoever it is to can it, but finishing Zuhr is more important. I begin reading out loud at the top of my lungs, scrunching up my eyes and letting my voice rise above the distracting music until I'm *singing* the way I always do when I'm reading the Qur'an out loud. I let the Arabic words take me far away, to another place, another country, another world.

I'm so involved that I don't even notice when the music stops and I'm still going at it. Only when I'm done praying does the peace and quiet register. *Thank God that's over.*

Then the door flies open and I'm face-to-face with Waleed, Bilal, and Matthew.

6

I stare at them staring at me kneeling on the ground. "Way to knock," I deadpan.

"Was that you?" Waleed asks.

I cross my arms. "Was what me?"

"You were singing," says Bilal.

"I was not *singing*. I was . . ." I mime bowing, feeling a little foolish.

"Oh," Waleed says. "But why were you reading out loud like that?"

"Because you guys were making so much noise and I couldn't even hear myself think!"

"Sorry, we didn't know anyone was in here," says Matthew. The front of his white shirt has a large Coke stain on it. "We have band class right after this, and Mr. Simmons and Ms. Grimes let us use the room to practice during lunch." These were some nice band teachers, renting out the room like some free Airbnb. Not good news for me.

"Why do you need to practice during lunch?" I ask.

Bilal laughs. It's a pleasant sound that almost makes me less irritated. Almost. "Summer vacation's over. That means a lot of homework and less time to practice after school."

True. It's only the first day of school and my agenda's pretty filled up with things to do.

Wait a minute—

I'm standing now, whirling on them with my hands on my hips. "It's only the first day of school," I retort. "You haven't even been to band yet. What were you practicing in there?"

"Oh, it's not for school," Waleed says. "We're practicing for our own band. Barakah Beats."

I blink. *Barakah* means "divine blessing" in Arabic. *Oh.* They're a Muslim boy band. That's . . . interesting. Obviously, my family's stance on music doesn't mean Muslim musical artists don't exist, but the topic can be a little awkward, or even downright ugly. The arguments I've read in the YouTube comments section under videos of Muslim musicians are . . . not nice.

So, I just shrug and say, "Cool. I can just pray first, then go to lunch on A days. Whatever." I make a move to leave, but the guys are still crowding the doorway. "Can you please move?"

Waleed puts up his hands. "Wait a minute. You have a nice voice," he says. "Like, a *really* nice voice. Where did you learn to recite like that?"

It takes me a second to answer because I wasn't expecting the compliment. "Well, I have the whole book memorized with tajweed." Tajweed are all the rules about how to properly pronounce and recite the Qur'an. It requires a lot of vocal practice and when you've got it down pat, it does sound like the person is singing.

Waleed's brown eyes light up. "You're a hafiza? My dad's a hafiz! Are you from Pakistan?"

"My grandparents are. I learned here, though. At Guided Light Academy. I just transferred."

"Oh, no wonder I didn't recognize you," says Matthew. "You're the first hijabi I've seen around school."

I look to Matthew in disbelief. "You're Muslim?"

"Yup. My parents converted when I was four. Yeah, I know. This face and the name Matthew Cohen don't really scream Muslim," he chuckles.

"We're not all the same," I say. Part of me is happy about meeting other Muslims at Farmwell, but the whole boy band thing makes me just as anxious to get away from them. "Um. It was nice meeting you guys, but I think the bell's about to ring—"

"Wait," Waleed says again. "Do you know Deen Squad?"

I crack a surprised smile. Boy, do I know Deen Squad. They used to be a duo who combined hip-hop with Islamic messages. I was so sad when they broke up. "I love Deen Squad."

Waleed exchanges looks with Bilal and Matthew. "Follow us," he says, and they shuffle back to the other room before I can respond. I consider ditching them to go to my locker and get my stuff for last block, but they seemed pretty excited about whatever they want to show me, and okay, I might be just a *little* bit curious.

When I walk into the main band room, Waleed's plugging his phone into the speakers. Matthew and Bilal stand at the ready beside him. They look like they're posing for a live-concert movie poster, all clear skin, side-swept hair, and star-studded smiles.

I freeze.

"Do you know this one?" asks Waleed. Before I can open my mouth, a track blares from the speakers and Bilal starts singing the opening verses to a song I recognize, one of Deen Squad's remixes. The one where they swapped the lyrics of Camila Cabello's "Havana" for "Madina." Waleed swings his shoulders like a puppet on the tempo's strings and Matthew joins in. The music bounds off the walls, reverberating in my ears. They sing like it's the most natural thing in the world, bouncing their heads to the rhythm, Matthew providing background vocals in perfect pitch. Their voices are mesmerizing.

I have to give it to them. They sound fantastic.

"Jump in!" Waleed shouts as the song reaches the last verse. My favorite part. I tap my hands on the back of a chair and, to my great surprise, I belt it out with them.

The all-Arabic outro rolls off my tongue just like all the times I've sung along while playing the song on repeat in my bedroom.

Then it's over. Everything is quiet again. We look around at one another, realizing that something has changed.

"Wow," I say.

"Are you guys thinking what I'm thinking?" Waleed asks his friends.

"That we rocked? Yeah!" Bilal exclaims. "We sounded so great! All thanks to— Oh. Shoot. We haven't even asked your name yet."

I blush. "Nimra."

"Nimra. That was lit, Nimra! Man, you should hang out with us. We'd love to have a girl in the band."

"So, we *are* thinking the same thing," Waleed says happily.

My legs turn to jelly. Hold up. There's no way they're *serious*. Me, join a band? Actively helping to create music? That crosses my boundaries. I've never gone against what I believe in before. Okay, I've definitely snuck a piece of candy during the day when I was little and first started fasting. But I felt bad afterward! Plus, Mama and Baba wouldn't approve if I joined the band either. They're strict about not going past the whole listening-to-music part. At weddings, my family and I are always one of the few who choose to sit out of all the dancing. Sometimes we leave before it even starts.

At the same time, I don't have it in me to just say no to the guys' offer. I might have to explain to them *why* and that's not exactly a good way to make new friends. Especially when Waleed, Matthew, and Bilal have been the only ones who've been kind to me all day. Even Jenna made me feel out of sorts in the cafeteria.

I try distracting them with a different topic. "So how big are you guys?"

"They played one of our songs at the school dance last year," Waleed says. "We weren't there, but people told us. That was a big deal."

Matthew gives Waleed a sideways look. "It's not like they played our song on the radio."

"Better than nothing!" says Bilal.

"Guys, look. I'm not really—"

"You don't have to sing if you don't want to," Waleed offers. "You can coach us. Help us with writing songs. Whatever you want." He sounds so sincere. He really wants me to say yes. Never in a million years would I have imagined that memorizing the Qur'an would make me stand out this way.

Just be yourself, Baba said.

But I can't afford to be myself. Not in middle school. Not if I want to make new friends.

It's not right. I should say no.

"I'll think about it," I tell them. Their eyes light up with hope and I hate that I gave it to them when I don't know what I'm going to do. I mean, I'm going to say no. I just have to think of a nicer way to tell them that.

"By the way, I have a question," I whisper to Waleed as we leave the band room. "Why did you help me on the math quiz earlier?"

Waleed shrugs. "Just being nice. And I didn't mean to look over at your paper. I just saw."

"I could've told on you and gotten you in trouble," I say.

"I know." Waleed taps me on the head playfully. "But I knew you wouldn't."

With that, he spins around and follows Bilal and Matthew toward House A. I stare after him, understanding why girls always say boys are confusing.

7

Jenna's back to her usual self when we walk home together after school. Her nose is glued to her phone, and she spends a solid five minutes choosing a filter on a picture I took of her modeling in front of a sycamore tree. I'm not sure if I want to get into social media. My parents think it's a waste of time, and since they made me promise not to "misuse" my phone . . .

"What do you think of this one?" Jenna asks, holding her phone with its cheetah-print case out to me.

"Pretty," I say. She hits post.

I keep replaying my encounter with Barakah Beats in my head, trying to convince myself it wasn't real. That I fell asleep while praying and dreamt the whole thing.

First-day-of-school jitters or something. I haven't told Jenna yet, and I don't know if I should. She wouldn't get why I didn't immediately say yes, but remembering how interested she was in Waleed, Matthew, and Bilal makes me want to spill the beans to impress her and have her think I'm just as cool as the other girls.

"—that true?"

I shake my head back to reality. "Sorry, what?"

Jenna looks at me strangely. "I said Julie told me you were sort of rude to her in homeroom. I told her there was no way. You don't have a mean bone in your body."

"Oh. That." I readjust my backpack straps as we walk through the park and tell her what actually happened.

Jenna's quiet for a moment. The late August heat is starting to make both of us sweat. "That was a pretty ridiculous thing for her to say. Sometimes Julie can be a ditz. But you didn't have to take it so personally, Nimra. She could've done better, but she was just trying to be nice."

I cut my eyes at Jenna. I can't tell whose side she's on. "I thought stereotyping wasn't nice?" I quip. "How would you feel if I called you a dumb blonde the first time we met?"

"But I'm not a dumb blonde."

"And I'm American."

"Okay, okay. You've made your point. I'll talk to Julie. How was the rest of your day?" Jenna drops her bag on the ground and claims a swing in the middle of the park. The same park where we met eight years ago. I join on the other seat. The urge to mention Waleed, Bilal, and Matthew is sitting at the tip of my tongue, but I swallow it back. Instead, I bring up something else eating at my brain. "Why were you ignoring me at lunch?"

"What?" Jenna snorts. "I was not. What made you think that?"

"Yes, you were. You barely spoke to me. It's like I was your little sidekick, not your partner in crime," I say.

"Nimra. Would you chill out? Real life is not a super-hero movie." Jenna kicks her legs up, lazily swinging back and forth. "Maybe you felt that way because you're used to how things worked at your old school. There were only two other people in your class that you talked to all the time. It's different here. You're still my friend even when I'm hanging out with other people."

I nudge the mulchy ground with my shoe. Her words soothe the burn I've been feeling since lunch. She's right, I guess. After all, we're here together at the park now. Maybe I was reading the situation all wrong and jumped to conclusions.

"Do you want to come over and have a snack with me before you go home?" I ask.

"Ugh, I wish. Coach is having us come in for practice every day. My team is trying to make championships this year."

"Man, do you ever catch a break?" I say.

"I dream about getting served in the face. Don't be surprised if you start seeing me diving around in the hallways." Jenna leaps off the swing and pretends to lunge for an imaginary volleyball with a stupefied look on her face. I laugh. Where was this side of her when we were at school?

Jenna stands, dusting her clothes off. "I gotta go get ready."

"Okay. See you tomorrow?"

"Mhm. And, Nimra? I think nerves really got to you at school today. We're cool, bud. Go home and have your snack. Sketch something. That always helps you." She waves goodbye in front of my house, and it takes all my strength to raise my hand back. Her comment sounded like it was supposed to be reassuring, but I got the sense that she was trying to brush the whole ignoring-me thing off like it was nothing. Now I'm annoyed that she won't take my feelings seriously.

*   *   *

Mama and Baba are both on the phone when I get home, so I sneak past them and head straight for the basement. It's the only place in the whole house they don't infest with their business stuff.

I take my hijab off on the sofa and run my fingers through sweat-slick hair. I insert earbuds into my phone, turn on an audio of the Qur'an I downloaded from iTunes, and open my sketchbook on my knees. I bite my pencil's eraser with Julie's words in my head. *I'll show you who's the* real *artist, Julie.* I start easy, a warm-up exercise like my teacher from my summer art program taught me. I trace my hand and doodle a henna design onto it. I started sketching when I was five. Mama bought me a set of pretty orange (my favorite color) pencils that had my name engraved on them and I didn't know what to do with them, so I just started drawing. And drawing. And kept drawing. One day, I want to be good enough to get into art school and become famous. Baba promised to buy me my own tablet one day when I'm a "pro." I'm not a pro yet, so I keep practicing. I've got time.

My mouth follows along from memory to the Qur'anic verses playing in my ear. Friends and family ask me all the time how on earth I managed to fit this entire book inside my head. One of my uncles likes to impersonate a volcanic eruption and say, "My head would explode!" I don't know. I just have a good memory.

I'm so distracted that I don't notice my parents sneak up behind me and almost make me pee my pants.

"Assalamu alaikum!" Baba shouts, shaking my shoulders. "Hey, kiddo!"

"We thought you'd be down here," Mama says, giving me a hug. They're still in their pajamas. Lucky ducks. "Sorry, we had to make a few calls when you got home. How was school? Did you make any friends? Did you wow the teachers with your brilliance?"

"Mama," I groan.

"Kidding. Okay, so tell us." Mama and Baba sit down on the carpet in front of me with their legs crossed like eager children waiting to hear a story.

I sigh, shutting my sketchbook. "It was all right," I say. "There are too many kids and too many teachers and too many classrooms. I got lost a few times. My teachers give too much homework."

"That's okay, beta. It's school!" says Baba. "Do you have any classes with Jenna?"

"PE tomorrow."

"And . . . was it okay? With her and the others? Did anyone bother you?" Mama asks.

Heat prickles my face. "Some people looked at me weird. Most people ignored me." Except Waleed, Bilal, and Matthew. They were the only ones who actually *saw* me. But I don't tell them that. It's not that they would freak out about me talking to boys. My parents aren't like that, but I'm afraid they're going to make a bigger deal out of it than it actually is. "I don't think anyone was trying to be mean, though."

"Of course not, Nimmy. No one knows you yet. It'll

take time. But when they do, they're going to see how amazing you are. They'll line up to be friends with you!" Baba kisses my forehead. "Come on. I could use a hand with dinner."

I follow Baba upstairs while Mama returns to work on the computer. She's a dud in the kitchen. Usually, she breaks or burns things and we have to gently kick her out. I wash my hands in the sink while Baba takes out a bowl of chicken he marinated overnight in the fridge. At our house, some days we eat pure Pakistani food and some days a mix of American and Pakistani. Never just American—too boring. We like to experiment with new recipes from YouTube.

My parents spend a lot of time with me compared with other parents in our family. I think they feel bad about me not having any brothers or sisters to play with. Mama went through a tough time after I was born and didn't want any more kids. All of Mama's friends' kids are way younger than me, and all my cousins are either too little (Mama's side) or live in Pakistan (Baba's side). Add that to going to a school where kids, especially the girls, were always coming and going, and voilà, you've got me—the oddball who doesn't fit in anywhere.

"I miss my old routine," I say while setting the table. It just comes out of my mouth. Mama and Baba look over at me, concerned. "I miss Sister Sadia."

"You'll see her again," Mama assures me. "And change is good. It takes time to get used to."

"I've been telling your mama to come out of her comfort zone for years, but she's so stubborn," Baba says jokingly. Mama tries to trip him as he walks by her.

I sit down to eat, my shoulders hunched.

"Nimra, give it a chance. If you're still unhappy in a couple of weeks, we'll work something out. Okay? Now please stop making that miserable face," says Mama.

"But what about Nano? I heard what she said to you at the party. She thinks I'm behind because I didn't go to public school."

Mama turns pale. "Saim! Are you hearing this? First the job thing and now this? I swear my parents are going to drive me to an early grave."

"Calm down, Maryam," Baba says. He puts his arms around Mama. "This isn't new. We've dealt with her comments for years, and we're not going to change the way we do things now."

"I don't get it." My eyes fly back and forth between Mama and Baba. "What's wrong with Mama not working outside the house, or me going to Islamic school?"

"Absolutely nothing," Baba says firmly. "We've just always done things differently than your grandparents, Nimra, because our priorities are different. They don't do it to be horrible. They want what's best for us, but they don't always know what that is. In their ignorance, sometimes they can really hurt our feelings. It was Mama's choice to leave the workforce to raise you, and Nano didn't like that, so sometimes she says things to make Mama regret it. Like what she said about you. Your nano's wrong," says Baba. "You are not behind in any shape or form and we didn't send you to public school because we think you 'need' it. It was just the right time. We know you're capable and we trust you to know right from wrong in your new environment."

Mama rests her elbow on the table and stabs at a piece of chicken, less cheery than she was a few minutes ago. I wanted to ask Mama for advice about Jenna but seeing her reaction to me bringing up Nano, I'm afraid it will only upset her more if she finds out my only friend snubbed me on my first day.

I don't know why Jenna turned into a completely different person around me at school, but I don't think I can handle it if she continues to do that. One minute she's hot, the next she's cold. It makes my head spin.

Then there's Barakah Beats's invitation to join the band. Even if I wanted to say yes, I couldn't tell Mama and Baba. They're mostly laid-back, but I know they won't approve of this. I can't even imagine what that would do to our relationship. If Mama and Nano are always arguing about Mama's choices, then could me joining Barakah Beats and going against Mama and Baba's beliefs do the same thing to us? Would they be so disappointed and angry with me that the three of us would turn into Mama and Nano 2.0?

The possibility makes fear flood my body. Yeah, there's no question. No band for me. I do *not* want that to happen to me and my parents. They're the most important people in my life. I can't let them down.

"Whatcha thinking so hard about, Nimmy?" I jerk my head up at Baba's voice like I've just been caught sneaking ice cream out of the freezer.

"Oh. Nothing. Just how much I don't want to do homework." I hope my voice hides my guilt.

At night, I slip into bed and put headphones in after flipping my sketchbook open to a new page. It's my nightly ritual. Even if it's just for a little bit, I can't sleep without creating. Tonight, I look up Barakah Beats on SoundCloud and listen to their music while I draw.

Starting a new picture is always intimidating, but I love it. There's so much to explore in the free-flowing lines. I start with rough scribbles, music notes popping up all over the page like twinkling stars as I nod my head to the catchy tune. At one point, I'm so distracted by singing along that my hand slips. One of the notes ends up looking like a wobbly letter *B*.

Suddenly, a neat little image forms in my head and I can't move my pencil fast enough. I test out different letterings with *B* turned into a music note. Once I pick one that I like, I turn to a clean page to draw two of them side by side and add more detail into the design, like stars. Then I rotate my sketchbook in my lap, refining the shapes with darker strokes. Barakah Beats plays in my ears while I concentrate.

After what feels like no time at all, I look up with drooping eyes and startle to see the hallway lights off. Yawning, I smile back down at my drawing.

At the completed band logo.

It took a lot of shading and line work, but in my opinion, it's one of my best yet. Now I'm officially ready to give the band my answer at school tomorrow. I hope gifting this to them makes my "no" hurt a little less for all of us. It sucks that I have to turn down the chance to make new friends.

As I slide under the covers, I think, *Whatever. I have Jenna. Once I get used to being in a new school, things will go back to normal between us.*

I fall asleep with my sketch pad next to me.

8

The next morning, I don't care about choosing the "right" outfit. I throw on all black with a checkered hijab and call it a day. Jenna frowns when she comes to pick me up. "When you're going to a funeral, but have a picnic at noon," she says. I *refuse* to laugh.

It's easier getting around school today. My first two blocks are pretty boring. Val's in my seventh-block science class and gives me a short nod. I stare off into space as Mrs. Nair goes over the syllabus. She tries to crack jokes to get us excited about lab safety, but we refuse to smile. That takes us until lunch, and we all push out from our chairs. I wonder if I should follow Val, but she practically runs out of the room with her lunch box before I can decide. Anyway, I forgot mine in my locker and have to go get it.

I blank on the second number in my combination and panic, eager to hurry it up so I can get a seat near Jenna in the cafeteria. I try three different numbers before getting the right one. My locker door slams open.

"Having a bad day?" asks a timid voice.

Khadijah is standing next to my locker, holding a green butterfly lunch box in front of her. I barely know her, but I'm happy to see her.

"Yeah, you could say that," I say, grabbing my lunch and the logo from the top shelf. I hold the half-folded piece of paper in front of my face, thinking one last time if I should do this.

"You came from Islamic school, right?" Khadijah falls into step beside me as we walk to the cafeteria. "My brother told me."

"Your brother?"

"Bilal."

"You're Bilal's sister?"

"I know. I'm the better-looking sibling."

I'm surprised how quickly Khadijah's made me laugh.

"He said you have an amazing voice and that they asked you to join their band. He wouldn't shut up about it last night." Khadijah's dark eyes sparkle as she says this. "You should do it."

"Why aren't you in it?" I say.

"I sound like a dead toad when I sing. I hated elementary school choir. And I don't play any instruments. I prefer books." Khadijah holds up the novel she's gripping in her other hand. *Amal Unbound* by Aisha Saeed. "I have a good ear, though. The band likes to use me as a sounding board for all their ideas. So, are you going to say yes?"

"I—" I've thought about it until my brain hurt. There's still a teeny tiny part of me that's holding back. Waleed, Matthew, and Bilal are three good-looking eighth-grade boys widely recognized at school. If I hang out with them, maybe Jenna will adjust easier to having me around at school.

But going against something that I believe in for popularity points? Using these boys—who seem really nice—for selfish reasons?

It's the most un-Islamic thought I've ever had.

Before I can answer Khadijah's question, we reach the cafeteria, and right there are Jenna and her friends, laughing and stealing one another's snacks and twirling their perfect hair like middle school princesses atop sporty thrones. Jenna's eyes flit up for half a second and I raise my hand to wave to her. She looks back down again.

She saw me. I know she did, but she's ignoring me. Like I'm nothing. A nobody.

My head feels hot. Hurt bubbles up inside me. I take a deep breath, in through my nose, out through my mouth. Then I turn around and march right out of the cafeteria.

"Where are you going?" Khadijah calls out, racing to keep up.

"I need to find the guys. I have something to tell them."

"Wait, Nimra." Khadijah catches my arm and pulls me to a stop. She's quite strong for her size. "Waleed's in study hall right now. In the auditorium." I stare at her questioningly. "I know all their schedules thanks to Bilal."

I look to the auditorium next to the lunchroom, at the backs of dozens of heads bent over their seats working.

"Good luck." Khadijah smiles like she's in on some secret and heads for the band room.

I inch toward the auditorium doors and peer inside. It's darker than in the hallways, but I can clearly see the faces of every eighth grader. Some of them have their headphones in or are scrolling on their phones. The teacher's doing the same up at his desk in front of the stage.

I finally spot Waleed's wavy black hair at the end of the third row. He's quietly tapping his feet and working on homework with his head down. If I only knew his number so that I could text him.

Wait!

I run to the band room right as Khadijah's standing up to pray. "Do you have Waleed's number? Would he mind if you gave it to me?"

"Sure." Khadijah reads it out loud for me from her phone.

"Thanks!" I jog back to the auditorium doors and type out a text to Waleed's number.

~~Hi, it's me!~~

~~Hey, this is Nimra! You heard overheard me~~
~~singing yesterday~~

~~What's up, Waleed?~~

Ugh, why is this so hard?

Hi, Waleed. It's Nimra. Khadijah gave me
your number. Can you come out of the
auditorium for a sec?

I hit send before I chicken out again and wait, biting
my tongue. Inside, Waleed checks his phone as the screen
lights up on his desk. My heart is thudding in my ears
so loud everyone can probably hear it. His eyes scan my
text and he immediately turns his head to see me creeping
outside the door. Waleed goes to the front of the room
with his agenda in hand. The teacher signs off on the hall
pass without even looking up.

"Hi," I say when he's joined me in the hallway.

"Hi," he says back. "Are you at lunch right now?"

"Yeah."

"Oh, bummer. We're not in the same lunch again."

I'm so glad he can't see my ears glow. I should've rehearsed what I was going to say because now all I can do is stare at him blankly. I didn't notice before, but Waleed dresses nicely. He's in a dark blue T-shirt, black jeans, and white sneakers today. I'm not used to being in school with boys, so I never really paid attention to them before. Sometimes I forgot boys my age existed. The fact that they're always around me now catches me off guard at random. Maybe it's normal to feel itchy around them. Right now I'm getting these jitters with Waleed that make me want to run and hide. It probably has to do with him being a celebrity at school—the face of the band—and me being, well, not.

Waleed rocks on his feet with his hands in his pockets. "So," he says slowly. "Have you thought about it?"

Silently, I hand him the half-folded piece of paper. Confused, he opens it. His eyes widen at the illustration.

"You drew this?" Waleed says in wonder. "That's amazing."

"It's for you. Actually, give it here. I forgot something."

I steal back the picture along with Waleed's pencil from between his agenda's spiral to make a quick adjustment before handing it back. He squints for a closer look at it and finally notices the small detail that I added. Their names were already in the byline. Now mine's included, too. He looks up at me hopefully.

"Is that a yes?"

"It's a yes." I smile, full of adrenaline and a smidge of anger for the way Jenna slighted me back there. "I'm in."

If Barakah Beats is as popular as everyone says they are, then maybe I can be cool enough for Jenna to want to sit with at lunch. It doesn't have to be for long. I'll only hang out with Barakah Beats until she's back on my side, then I can nicely tell the guys I want out.

It's just a *small* lie.

I've never lied about anything before. Okay, this one time Baba asked me if his new haircut looked good, and I told him it did when it was actually pretty ugly. But I have to fix whatever is going on with Jenna lately, and joining Barakah Beats is the key. Mama and Baba can't ever know. They definitely won't like the part about me lying to them either, but if my plan works, they'll never have to find out. I'll get my friend back, and my parents will keep being proud of how awesome I am. Everyone wins.

Waleed opens his mouth in a silent scream and pumps his fist. He gives me a high five. "Awesome! I can't wait to tell Bilal and Matthew." He waves my drawing around in the air like it's a prize. "Aw, man, I really wish we had lunch together both days. Oh well. We'll figure it out."

"Yeah. Sure," I say, nodding like a song stuck on repeat. "Just wanted to let you know. I should go. I still have to eat and read Zuhr."

"Okay, see you in the band room tomorrow? I've got your number now, too."

He does, and the realization sends butterflies through my stomach. I give him two thumbs up and start to walk away.

"Hey, Nimra," Waleed says, and I look over my shoulder. "I think it's cool you make time for namaz during school. The three of us were saying how we wished we were more like you and Khadijah." Waleed flashes one last grin and disappears back into the auditorium.

Those were the last words I imagined anyone at this school would say to me. I don't realize how much I needed to hear them until I go to prepare for namaz with a little more skip in my step, humming as I rinse my feet under water. Today, I don't care if someone catches me.

9

Julie is in eighth-block PE with me and Jenna. It's *so* awkward.

Mr. Peters—or Geezers Peters, as the students like to call him—spends the first thirty minutes assigning us lockers and uniforms. I, of course, tell him that I can't wear shorts for religious reasons and have to bring sweatpants from home. I also make it a point to not change in front of the other girls and call dibs on the bathroom stall. At least I have PE last so that I don't have to sit in another class stinking like a skunk.

Even though we don't begin any real activities, Mr. Peters still takes us outside for "fresh air" and makes us walk around the track. The sun is blazing overhead, and I think I might die.

Jenna and Julie are walking together ahead of me, whispering about something. Jenna finally notices when I start to fall behind. She looks over her shoulder at my reddened face. "You can roll up your sleeves and pants to cool off," Jenna says.

"Actually, direct sun exposure makes you even hotter," I pant. "That's why men and women in the Middle East wear long, flowing clothes."

Julie stares at me like I'm a dead bug she found in her shoe. She takes Jenna by the arm and starts to face her forward again when Bilal comes out of nowhere and throws his arms around me. I stagger onto the grass.

"Waleed told us the good news!" he says excitedly. "I'm so stoked!"

"Dude, let her breathe." Matthew's here, too. They must be in the other class. PE blocks are so big, consisting of sixth, seventh, and eighth graders, that I didn't notice them in the gym earlier.

I push Bilal away with a pointed look.

"Oh, crap! Right. Boundaries," Bilal says sheepishly. "Sorry, Nimra."

"It's okay. Just don't do it again."

People are definitely staring at us now. Some of the older boys are hooting. Very mature. Jenna and Julie stop ten feet away, wearing twin expressions of shock. Matthew helps me stand, and Julie's face twists like she drank expired milk.

I lower my voice, for some reason not ready to publicly declare my new affiliation. "So, what's the plan? Do I need an official membership card?"

Matthew laughs. "Nah. Just come to the band room during lunch tomorrow. Waleed said he has something important to tell us."

"Apparently it's going to grow our image," Bilal adds, smiling wide. "We'll see. Wanna walk with us? You're part of the group now. We want to get to know you."

I should be ecstatic that they want to spend time with me, but hanging out with them is going to draw even more attention. I don't want to make a scene. The other boys are still making wildlife sounds, and it's starting to get annoying.

"Can we talk later? I have to, um, use the bathroom really quick."

Jenna's at my side in a flash once Bilal and Matthew are gone. "What was that about? What did they say to *you*?"

I ignore her insulting tone. "He was just apologizing for running into me."

"That's it? No way. There's more. You guys were talking like friends."

I narrow my eyes at her. "It's called being nice."

My implication goes right over Jenna's head. "Is there something you aren't telling me?"

Out of the corner of my eye, I see Julie standing with her arms crossed, wearing an exasperated look on her face. She's staring at the group of eighth graders. More specifically, she has her gaze on the sandy-haired boy with brown eyes now piggybacking Bilal around the track.

Oh.

"Does Julie have a crush on Matthew?" I wonder out loud.

Jenna shushes me like I just spilled some big government secret. "Don't say that out loud!" she hisses. "And don't tell anyone! It's against girl code."

I hold up my hands in surrender while a thought crosses my mind. Julie's crush makes all of this even better than I thought. Now they'll be even more impressed—or *jealous*, in Julie's case—when they find out about me joining the band! "My lips are sealed. He is cute, though."

Jenna raises her eyebrows at me. "Don't even think about it. Julie's been in love with Matthew since third grade." Holy smokes. "Obviously, the competition is harder since the three of them started the band. But Julie's too shy to go up to him."

Barakah Beats is like an exclusive club everyone wants to be a part of, and I lucked out by some freak accident. I admit I'm enjoying how in awe Jenna is of me for just talking to them. What if she knew the truth? Everyone's going to find out at some point, and Jenna should find out on *my* terms.

"He's really nice. I talked to him and Bilal once before," I say casually.

Jenna freaks like I just told her I had lunch with the president. "What? How? Where? When? Why didn't you tell me?"

"I was going to find you at lunch, but you were a little busy." I shrug like, *'Twas your fault*, then whisper in her ear, "The guys asked me something."

"OMG, what?" Jenna looks ready to launch herself into the air like a rocket from the suspense.

"Tell you tomorrow at lunch." That will make sure she saves me a seat in the cafeteria. It also means Julie, Evelyn, and Val will be there to see her reaction. I'm a genius. "Now if you'll excuse me. I have to pee." I duck around her and run toward the school building, feeling victorious when Jenna complain-screams behind me. *That should keep her head buzzing.*

10

"Nimmy, what about this?" Baba picks up a protractor and examines it like he's never seen one before.

When I told my parents I needed to go school supply shopping, I meant Target, not the makeshift store Farmwell sets up in its library after school during the first whole week of classes. But Mama and Baba wanted an excuse to visit Farmwell. Baba's already been distracted three different times. It's like he's the one in middle school and I'm the parent who just wants to go home ASAP.

"I don't need that." I show him the seventh-grade supply list again. "I'm in algebra, not geometry."

Baba puts the protractor back. I push him toward a table of binders before he gets away from me a fourth time. Mama found someone she knows and they've been talking near the library's checkout desk since we got here. I keep a firm hand on Baba's shirt while I pick out different colored binders to add to the basket, but stop when I notice the table section labeled for Art 6, 7, and 8, displaying fine-tip Sharpie markers, Prismacolor colored pencils, and packets of drawing paper. Everything else in the room disappears and I gravitate toward the art supplies like a child bribed with treats.

I gesture to get Baba's attention, to say, *Look at all this cool stuff! Oh wait, you didn't let me take art so they're not on my list*, but someone else beats me to it.

"Saim! Is that you?" Baba turns at the sound of his name and beams at the gentleman in a white thobe heading our way.

"Usman bhai!" says Baba. They shake hands and hug. "What are you doing here? I thought your son was in college?"

"I have another son in the eighth grade. He's around here somewhere with his mother. I lost them between highlighters and folders."

"Usman bhai, this is my daughter, Nimra." Baba nudges me gently toward his friend. I nod politely.

"Assalamu alaikum. Ah, yes. Our newest hafiza, mash Allah." Brother Usman smiles. "My son Waleed has told me all about you."

My blood runs cold at the same time Baba's proud grin slips. "You know him?" Baba asks, looking down at me. "You didn't mention that."

"We have algebra together," I say, but alarms are going off in my head. Did Waleed tell his dad about me joining the band? *Please God, don't bring it up to Baba.*

"He tells us you have a magnificent voice. We'll have to hear it one day," says Brother Usman.

Just then, I spot Waleed and his mother through a gap between shoppers over at the register. Waleed turns around to look for his father, and that's when he sees me and Baba. His face lights up. I'm this close to having an aneurysm when he comes over to join us.

"Hey!"

"Hi," I say faintly.

"Assalamu alaikum, Uncle," Waleed says to Baba. Everyone in our culture is Uncle or Auntie, regardless of blood relations.

"Waalaikumusalam. I like your shirt." Waleed's in a

Starboy Panther T-shirt. It's a reference to The Weeknd, but I don't think Baba knows that.

"Thank you." Waleed stands taller. "I want to be a musician, too, when I grow up."

I do *not* like where this is going.

Brother Usman puts his arms around his son affectionately. "You can be whatever you want after you become an engineer. Just work hard."

Waleed rolls his eyes so that only I can see. He doesn't say anything after that. My breathing returns to normal when Brother Usman says that they should get going and he hopes to see us around. Waleed waves at me as they leave the library.

"Interesting," Baba muses on our way to the car.

"What's interesting?" Mama asks as she helps me with the shopping bags.

"That someone like Usman bhai's son wants to be a musician. It's funny how some kids grow up to be so different from the way their parents raise them."

My stomach flips, and Mama says, "You're looking at a good example of what that looks like right in front of you. Sometimes going against your parents' wishes is the right thing to do."

Baba starts the engine. "Yes, but some things in particular . . . it's tough. How do you let your child do something you don't agree with, but explain it in a way that doesn't turn them away from you? We've seen it, Maryam. Parents and children who cut each other off because of differences in opinion. I'd be heartbroken if we were in a situation like that with Nimmy. It's not like we can just go with *whatever* she wants."

Hello, I'm sitting right here! I want to say, but too many thoughts are whooshing through my head and none of them are good. Would my parents be that upset with me if I chose a different path from theirs? Mama did it and look where that got her with Nano. I thought my parents were more understanding, but I guess they have their breaking point, too.

What if Mama and Baba never trust me again if they find out about me and Barakah Beats?

"Well, we all have big dreams when we're young," Mama says. "I'm sure Usman bhai's son will come around."

"Yes, but should Usman bhai be treating it so lightly in the first place? Seems like setting Waleed up to be let down. Parents need to keep their kids' best interests at heart, even if it means tough love."

"Does that include *not* letting them take the subjects they want?" I say quietly from the back seat, my hands clenched in my lap. I'm selfishly using the conversation to help myself more than to defend Waleed.

"What's that, now?" Mama asks in the rearview mirror.

Baba sighs. "She was looking at the materials students need for art class."

"Stuff I can't use because I'm not in it!"

"That's no problem. We can just buy you the same supplies to use at home," Mama says, like that solves everything.

"Are you going to hire a teacher for me the whole year, too?"

"Nimra," Baba says, a warning in his voice. "Not this again."

"This isn't fair," I gripe, crossing my arms. "It feels like you don't support my dreams."

"Nimmy, that's ridiculous," says Mama. "Besides not

letting you take it in school, haven't we always encouraged your art? So much, in fact, that you're hung up on this *one* thing we didn't let you do. You can't have everything in life."

I'm too mad to talk to them the rest of the way home. Instead, I stare out the window and fearfully mull over Baba's remark about the musician thing. I have to work my magic fast before Mama and Baba catch on to my lie. I've joined the band, and now all I have to do is stick it out until my friendship with Jenna is back on solid ground. I won't need long to impress her with my new connections. A week should cut it. That should be enough time for Jenna to realize that, with or without Barakah Beats, I'm still the same Nimra she's always known. And the band shouldn't grow to rely on me that quickly. We'll only need to have a few rehearsals—then they can go back to how they were.

11

Waleed's leg bounces eagerly underneath the table all through algebra. He keeps throwing me glances and smiling and I don't know what to make of it.

He waves his friends ahead and waits for me when lunch finally rolls around. After Jenna suddenly turned on me, part of me believed Waleed wouldn't want anything to do with me outside of band meetings and that his friendliness from last night was just a result of our dads being there.

"You ready?" he asks. He taps his fingers on the desk. The itch inside him to share whatever news he has can't wait any longer.

I totally get it because I've been dying to share *my* news

with Jenna since yesterday. She's tried everything in her power to get me to open up ever since I put the Barakah Beats thing in her ear in PE—even chased me around the park on our way home, threatening to sue me—but I held my ground for the sake of timing.

I grab my things and follow Waleed to the cafeteria. I feel like every pair of eyes swings in our direction as we enter. I scour the room and locate Jenna and her gang at the same table from before. The girls look as if someone slapped them all right across the face when they see me standing at the popular eighth-grade boys' table.

Jenna opens her mouth and I hold one finger up to her like *Wait for it.*

"Eat fast, guys," Waleed orders. "Then let's go straight to the band room. We have a lot to talk about."

"Aw, come on. I'm hungry." Bilal pats his stomach. "Let me *enjoy* my food."

One of the boys whose name I don't know fixates on me. "Who's the new girl?"

"This," Bilal says, introducing me with a flourish, "is Nimra. Say hello to the fourth member of Barakah Beats, everyone! Can't wait till you all get to hear her sing. If you think I'm good, she's a natural. And you know I'm a big fan of me." His voice is loud enough to carry over another table in every direction. Jenna's, Val's, and Evelyn's eyeballs are bugging out of their sockets. Julie has actual murder on her face when Matthew leads a round of applause.

I hide my face behind my lunch box but can't resist curtsying. The reactions from Jenna's table are priceless.

"Let me know when it's time to go," I tell Waleed before heading in that direction. Jenna snatches me by the shoulders and plops me down on the bench.

"This is what you've been keeping from me?" says Jenna. "Nimra! How could you? I thought we told each other everything! They invited you to join their *band*? How did this happen?" Val and Evelyn lean forward to hear, too. Even Julie's curiosity is showing despite her steely eyes on me, but I'm not flinching underneath them today.

I tap my chin in fake contemplation. "Hmm, where do I start?"

Jenna punches my arm semi-hard. "You're evil. Spill already. Don't leave anything out."

I recap what happened on the first day of school in the

band room. I didn't know I was bursting to tell her until I'm almost out of breath at the end of my story.

"I can't believe you didn't tell me," Jenna says exasperatedly after I finish. "You don't keep things like that from your best friend. How did I not know you could sing?"

"I know, right? I didn't either."

"You should give us a live performance," says Jenna. "Start a number at school like in all the musicals." She swings her shoulders in a funny jig to demonstrate.

"Ugh, no way. You know I don't do that," I say.

"Right. I forgot about your family's no-dancing rule," says Jenna. I should probably explain to her that it's more than just about not dancing, but the less she understands, the fewer questions she'll have about why I'm going against my religious beliefs.

Val tilts her head in the direction of the boys' table. "So, you're, like, friends with them now?" she asks me. If possible, Julie tenses even more at her question. I have to keep myself from smiling smugly at her across the table.

I act like it's nothing, but inside, their awe is giving me life. "Kind of."

Jenna's eyes sparkle like blue gemstones. "Nimra, do you know what this means? You're on your way to becoming a celebrity! Next thing we know, your face will be everywhere! Just imagine." She sweeps her hand in the air in front of us dramatically. "Billboards. A hit album. Sold-out concerts. TV interviews—"

"Bobbleheads!" Evelyn adds.

"Whoa, whoa, slow down!" I laugh at the prospect of Barakah Beats bobbleheads. "Let me, like, actually be in the band for more than a day."

"Trust me. You guys are gonna be a sensation," Jenna says.

"Did I hear 'sensation'? You're talking about us, right?" Bilal comes up behind me with Waleed and Matthew. Julie almost chokes on her turkey sandwich. The other three snap upright.

I give Bilal a witty grin. "Duh."

"We love to know it," he says.

"Sensations have to put in the work," says Waleed. "Come on, Nimra. We're going to the band room now."

"She's all yours," Jenna says sweetly. She tugs on my sleeve as I get up to leave. "I wanna hear all about it after school," she whispers. Triumph fills me up like helium in a balloon. I give her my word before Waleed ushers us all out of there impatiently.

Once we're in the band room, Waleed wastes no time. He claps his hands together and says, "ADAMS is having a fundraiser in the beginning of October. They're raising money by hosting a talent show. The winner gets free tickets to Six Flags!" ADAMS is our community's local mosque and one of the biggest in the country. It has satellite locations throughout Northern Virginia, but the main branch is the hub of all activity. I did Hifz at one of the smaller locations because it's the only one that has a teacher for the girls' Hifz program. "This is it!" Waleed continues. "We've been wanting to do a live show forever, and now we have the chance to perform in front of our entire community! My mom says we have to sign up before all the spaces are gone."

Bilal and Matthew leap up and start talking over each other excitedly. My sputtering brain drowns them out. I start to feel nauseous. This has to be a joke. Me? *Sing to music?* In front of hundreds of people? How am I supposed to explain that to Mama and Baba? No. Forget my parents. This doesn't sit right with *me*. It's one thing to fake participation for just a little while, but I can't do a live show!

Waleed's eyes dance with joy. "All the proceeds are going to refugee families," he says. "I was thinking we could write an original for them instead of doing a remix. Something to give them hope about starting a new life. We have a little more than a month. I think we can pull it off."

"That's a great idea," Bilal agrees. He snaps his fingers. "Hey, what if we finished that one song from last year? We can change up the lyrics, and it'll save us some time."

Matthew hums a gentle-toned melody. "That one?"

"Yeah. You still have it?" Bilal asks.

"It's probably somewhere in my room," says Waleed. "I'll check."

"It still needs a lot of work." Matthew thumbs his chin, looking at the ground. "It'll be hard. We'll have to meet more often. There's not enough time at school. Hey, lookie who's here."

Khadijah enters the band room and I'm so relieved to see her I might cry. Even though her being here's not going to change Waleed's mind about the talent show, her presence is still a comfort compared with the dread in my stomach. Khadijah sits down next to me. "Sorry I'm late."

Bilal pokes his sister's side. "What are you doing here?"

"Waleed invited me. So, what's up?"

Waleed fills her in on the ADAMS fundraiser. "Oh, cool!" Khadijah says. "That sounds like fun. What do you need me to do?"

"What you're good at. Being our VIP audience. Making sure we sound fantastic and telling us when we don't."

Khadijah leans forward. "Really?"

"Yes." Waleed smiles.

I'm so screwed.

Matthew opens the Notes app on his phone, typing and talking at the same time. "Khadijah—coach. Waleed—synth program/keyboard. Matthew—guitar. Bilal—lead vocals. Nimra—" Matthew lingers on my name, looking up at me with soft eyes. "Lead vocals."

Shoot. Maybe I can make up some kind of story to get out of this whole thing.

But I already told Jenna! I can't be, like, *Just kidding* literally five minutes later, especially after seeing how shocked and delighted she was at me joining the band. Jenna sounded like her old self for a minute there. I'll lose whatever chance I gained to make things right with her. I just need a little more time to show her that I'm a new and improved, much cooler version of the girl she used to ride bikes and save the world with. This is worth it.

I also like the Barakah Beats boys and Khadijah. I don't want to stop hanging out with them before I've really had a chance to become friends with them.

One side of Waleed's lips turns up. "Everyone's on the same page, right? We all agree to do this?"

Bilal, Matthew, and Khadijah shout their approval so loudly, no one notices my silence.

Waleed passes the sign-up sheet around. I get it last, and I read everyone's names. Waleed Syed. Matthew Cohen. Bilal Mohamed. Khadijah Mohamed. None of them notice my hand hesitate over the clipboard. They're too absorbed in planning talks.

The only way for me to win is to not stay in the band long enough to make it to the talent show. Once I figure things out with Jenna in a few days, I'll be out. I'll make sure Barakah Beats won't need me in the end, I tell myself as I write down my name.

Waleed slips the forms into his backpack and shoulders it.

"There's no way our team won't win." Waleed says it like he believes it. "We got this. Starting Friday, it's go time."

The end-of-lunch bell rings right on cue. At the same time, I remember that I haven't prayed Zuhr yet. I grab my things and bolt from the room to squeeze it in before last block. I don't know what it is that makes my legs tremble while I stand in the direction of Mecca, but I can't shake the feeling of impending doom.

What have I gotten myself into?

12

Friday's the first time I'm missing Jummah prayer for as long as I can remember. Instead of being at the masjid squishing my toes together on the plush carpet and listening to the imam give the Friday khutbah, I'm stuck listening to Ms. Yariks drone on about order of operations. As if Dear Aunt Sally is going to help me in the Afterlife.

I can tell some of the other kids are already lost, but no one asks Ms. Yariks to slow down or clarify. It's the Friday funk. Waleed looks half-asleep at his desk. I pinch his elbow once, making him jerk. When he lifts his head, I see that he's been scribbling lyrics on the back of the assessment we took on the first day of school. I got a 100, but know I don't deserve it.

Waleed starts to lose focus again and I reach over to subtly slide his paper over to me. *You can't be an engineer if you sleep through math*, I write.

Waleed looks at it, sighs, and jots back, *I don't want to be an engineer.*

Why not? My dad's an engineer. He was, at least. Now he and my mom run a business.

Because I don't like it. I want to make music, he replies. Waleed taps his pencil against his lips and adds, *What about you? Do you want to be an artist?*

Since I got him to wake up, we should stop passing notes before Ms. Yariks catches us, but it seems rude to just leave him hanging. *Yep. I didn't have any cousins my age to play with growing up, so I was always in a corner by myself at family events. One day I just started doodling all over napkins and haven't stopped.*

Haven't stopped drawing on napkins? Waleed jokes.

No, you fool. Drawing in general. I freak out that I might have gone too far with the fool comment, but Waleed just smirks at my handwriting.

How are you with words? he asks. *Can you look over what we have so far for the song? There's more, but I wrote them down in a notebook at home and forgot to bring it today.* Waleed underlines the part he wants me to check and passes the note back to me. He writes big and we're running out of room, so I flip my notebook to a new page. The lyrics are good, but when I read them, I'm not hooked. Shouldn't I feel something, even without the music?

I think about it for a moment. It's a song about refugees, but the lyrics are all about us, here. *It doesn't feel like we're including the refugees in the song,* I write. *What if it switches from our perspective to theirs?*

Waleed sucks in a quick breath. *Why didn't I think of that? Maybe it can be more like a conversation! Can't wait to share with the rest of the group. Thanks! We make a good team. :)*

If he only knew what a rotten team member I actually am. I shouldn't have helped him so easily. I should have pretended like the lyrics were okay and let Bilal, Matthew, or Khadijah do the critiquing.

"Guys," Ms. Yariks breaks in, and we all jump. I cover our notes with my arms. But Ms. Yariks is addressing the entire class. "Wake up, y'all. I know it's almost the weekend, but I have you here for twenty more minutes. What is the answer to this question?" She points to the equation on the screen projector. I hear a couple of students shift in their seats, but there are no volunteers.

I decide to save us in case Ms. Yariks is the type of teacher who believes in homework over the weekend. I raise my hand and she calls on me. "The answer is eighteen. Add up the numbers in the parentheses, take the square root, then subtract."

"Very good, Nimra," says Ms. Yariks. "Glad to know somebody was paying attention. Also, if anybody needs help, you can go to her. Nimra's the only one who got a one hundred on the assessment."

Waleed winks at me. I turn my eyes down, smiling despite myself.

When I check my phone before lunch, there's a text from Jenna waiting for me.

Saved you a seat!

The message shoots a thrill through me. I almost run out the door to find Jenna in person, but then I remember my next few A-day lunch blocks are booked. Should've thought that one through. At least my B-day lunch blocks are free to hang out with her.

> **Me:** Sorry, I have plans with the band.
> **Jenna:** Ah! Okay, international superstar .
> **Me:** Today's our first rehearsal. Wish me luck! Tell you all about it later!
> **Jenna:** Good luck! So, the guys really ARE your friends now?

Waleed packs up his things while chatting with a couple people in his class about a civics quiz they have next block. He doesn't have to beg like a sad puppy to be included. His friends actually want to hang out with him.

They're my bandmates, I respond at the same time Waleed appears at my elbow, ready to walk me out as usual. *Temporarily, at least.*

*   *   *

I try to make sense of the music sheets spread out before me on the stand. *Am I supposed to know how to read this? What does any of this even mean?*

Matthew clears his throat. "I know it's kind of a mess right now. I played around with a new sound. It's a work in progress." It looks more like he didn't have an eraser sitting around.

Waleed looks like his head is about to explode. "Wait a minute. You didn't tell us you started working on the music already!"

"Yes, I did," Matthew counters. "If you'd paid attention to my text last night. I sent it to all of you. Sorry I didn't include you, Nimra. I didn't have your number."

"We don't even have the song written yet! What if the words and the music don't go together? We'd be wasting time and doing twice the work." Waleed rakes his hand down the side of his face.

Matthew folds his arms, frowning. "You're the one who wants us to rewrite this whole song *and* rehearse it *and* perform it in just one month. I was just trying to help by getting ahead."

"You guys agreed to do it, too!" Waleed half yells.

"Both of you shut up and have some baklava," says Bilal. "We can't work on empty stomachs." Apparently, his and Khadijah's mom is a master chef. They brought a tray of her homemade dessert and were unwrapping the foil at the teacher's desk. Khadijah takes out a single square and brings it to me on a napkin. The rich, syrupy sweet melts in my mouth like heaven.

Waleed slumps down in a chair. "Not hungry."

"Dude, come on." Bilal nudges Waleed's leg. "We're all here now. Have some sugary goodness and loosen up."

"Bilal's right," I say. "Stressing out won't do any good. We just have to organize better. From now on, none of us does anything without letting the others know."

"I did let him know," Matthew grumbles.

Waleed still looks pretty grumpy with Matthew even though he has baklava in his hand—sweets are supposed to make everything better. I get why Waleed's upset. He obviously takes the whole band thing seriously, but a leader shouldn't ever lose his cool. Sometimes I want to rip my drawings to shreds for not being good enough. I would have quit sketching a long time ago if I never gave myself a chance to practice and get better. Memorizing the Qur'an taught me a lot about patience. It's not easy to do at all.

I didn't really plan on helping with the song anymore. I wanted to watch the guys do their thing with minimal interference, but since no one else is stepping up to take the reins, I figure it won't hurt to give them a *small* push.

"Let's hear it." I pull up a chair next to Khadijah. We create a circle that Matthew closes after sitting down with his guitar. "Waleed, do you have the lyrics you were working on?" I ask.

"I haven't made the changes to it yet," he says.

"That's okay. Let me see it anyway."

Waleed hands me the piece of paper and I borrow a clipboard to set it against my lap with one hand. The baklava made my fingers all sticky. I nod at Matthew. "Go ahead."

Matthew wiggles his fingers, lowers his eyes in concentration, and starts playing. He strums out a steady mid-tempo acoustic, tapping one foot along to the beat. He twists his fingers up and down the fretboard like it's an extension of his hand. It's completely different from Barakah Beats's usual hip-hop/rap sound. The melody echoes from a quiet place in a world torn apart. It has the ability to fix broken hearts and ignite hope. We all listen, entranced. Matthew stops playing, but the song stays with me like a pleasant dream after waking up.

An amazed laugh escapes Bilal. "Ho-ly. It's so different from the original. How did you come up with that?"

"All I did was change it from major to minor scale," Matthew explains.

"You haven't come up with something that good in a long time," says Khadijah.

Matthew shoots her a look. "Thanks?"

"I love it," says Waleed. "It's not too slow or too upbeat. And I have some ideas of what the keyboard will sound like with it."

"I think we should release a teaser and get feedback. We haven't uploaded anything new since the summer," Bilal says. "Everyone'll be so excited."

Matthew hugs his guitar to his chest protectively. "It's not ready yet." I smile in sympathy. I'm the same way about showing my sketches to anybody before they're done—or ever.

I consider the sheet in front of me. "Can you play that

first part again?" I ask Matthew. He does and I uncap a pen with my teeth to cross out lyrics and rewrite new ones. "And the next part." I block out all other noise to focus on the rhythm. We repeat until the sheet music runs out and I have a two-stanza poem, "verses" in music. I scoot over to Bilal and hold out the sheet between us. "Now we're going to add vocals while he plays. You sing the welcomer's parts, and I'll sing the refugee's."

I listen with my ears trained open as our voices combine in turn with Matthew's guitar. It takes almost no effort for us to sync. Bilal has a strong, unwavering voice. Mine is the perfect complement. Our notes soar through the air. I tap my knee in time to the beat, forgetting everything except for the music. We reach the end and the guitar cuts off. Matthew's lips part in astonishment.

"I have goose bumps," breathes Khadijah.

Waleed is gaping at us like all his dreams came true. "How did you come up with that so fast?" he asks. "It takes me days to do the same."

I shrug. I'm surprised at how easily the lyrics came to me, too. I never thought I'd be good at writing, but all it took was filling the music in with the right words, like adding details to a sketch once I have the outline in front of me. After that, it's just a matter of toying with it until the right techniques bring it to life.

"We basically have everything up to the pre-chorus," Matthew says, finally perking up.

"I should just burn the notebook I have at home and let Nimra write the rest," Waleed laughs, also in a much better mood.

"Fine. But I'm taking all the credit," I joke.

"Why not?" Waleed asks, suddenly serious. "You're one of us now. You take credit where it's yours."

My chest tightens. *Nimra, you ding-dong! You're not supposed to be showing off to them! Why did you have to open your big mouth in the first place?* I didn't mean to get side-tracked, but it all just came so naturally. It's kind of like when you're so determined to have a bad time that you accidentally end up having a good time instead. The guys are really talented, and I'm surprised how easy they are to be around given how hard it's become to be myself while hanging around Jenna.

Our progress today improves everyone's mood, including Waleed's. I get to sit there for the rest of lunch and listen to the guys run through some of their old songs for fun. I've been listening to Barakah Beats's music the last couple of days while doing homework, so I'm able to sing along.

I've never been part of a creative group before. A band wouldn't have been my first choice, but feeling wanted trumps feeling guilty by a little. Even though I'm not being true to myself. Even though I don't want to be making music when it burns like a fire in my mind.

We're doing a good thing, I convince myself. We're helping to raise money for refugee families. For people who are really in need. Does one wrong thing cancel out another good thing? Our niyyah—intentions—are what matter, and they aren't bad.

I just have to hang in there for a little longer. So far, Jenna's been focused on wanting to talk about me and the band, but I don't want our friendship to be all about that. Maybe I'll ask her to hang out this weekend, and instead of gossiping about Barakah Beats, we'll talk about everything else like we used to. Then I can abort this whole mission once Jenna remembers I'm more than just Nimra and The Band.

I stare off into space while the others eat and talk happily around me until Khadijah tugs on my sleeve. "Wanna pray now?"

Another wave of guilt hits me. I forgot about Zuhr again.

I nod and we go over to the other room after making wudu. Khadijah takes a scarf out of her bag and puts it on. She looks adorable in it.

"You look cute," I tell her.

"Thanks!" Khadijah spins gracefully like a dancer. Her black, white, and golden scarf fans out around her face. "My parents brought it back for me from Hajj. It's the only one I like praying in."

"I have a Qur'an like that! It's got pink-sprayed edges. My mom gave it to me to do Hifz with."

"When did you start wearing hijab? When you started Hifz?" asks Khadijah.

"No, two years ago," I say, laying out a prayer rug for us to share. "I was always in it for school, and then I just wore it everywhere. Okay, and *maybe* I was too lazy to do my hair. Like, now I can go three days without a shower, and no one will know. Unless I smell!" I say as Khadijah busts out laughing. "But now my intentions are better. Swear!"

"That was you?" Bilal teases, poking his head into the room. He sniffs the air suspiciously. "I knew I smelled something funky."

"Hey, no eavesdropping!" Khadijah says.

"You're supposed to be praying. But since you're not yet, question. What famous singer does Nimra sound like? We can't agree."

I blush when Khadijah says, "That's easy. She reminds me of Demi Lovato."

"See, Waleed! I told you she's too good to be Taylor Swift!"

"You really think I sound like Demi?" I ask Khadijah when Bilal leaves.

"Yup. Just younger. Your voice could be their voice's little sister."

I straighten the prayer rug with my socked foot even though it doesn't need to be fixed. "You're just being nice."

"Nuh-uh. I can't sing, but I'm really good at listening. You've got a fantastic voice."

Hearing Khadijah say that brings back some of the energy I lost earlier for feeling bad about helping the band. I leave it at that, though, because I don't want to say something that might tip Khadijah off about what's really going on inside my head. If there's one person in the group I don't want to disappoint, it's her.

We finally pray in quiet unison.

13

On Saturday afternoon, I burst through the doors of my old school and head straight for Sister Sadia's classroom. She makes a delighted sound at my entrance and throws her arms around me. I hug Sister Sadia tight, sure I'm never letting go. "You have no idea how happy I am to see you," I gush.

"I'm happy to see you, too, my little tiger. I miss you so much." Sister Sadia calls me by that nickname because my name means "female tiger" in Arabic. She looks down at me with love. Sister Sadia is Egyptian. She's old, but not too old, and her hijab always ends in a triangle point above her forehead.

"She made us drive all the way out here for namaz

instead of the masjid near our house. On a weekend. Just to see you," Baba tells her.

Sister Sadia gives a gap-toothed smile. "I'm honored. How's middle school?" she asks when Baba leaves to join the congregation on the men's side.

"It's horrible," I exaggerate. "They make us run the mile in the intense sun and give us a gajillion homework problems and if Mama or Baba forget to make me lunch, I have to eat greasy pizza."

Sister Sadia mock shivers. "Sounds like enormous pressure. Are you making any new friends?"

"It's only been a week," I say, hoping she doesn't ask more questions about that.

"I know it's tough," says Sister Sadia. "But you had to get out there at some point." I look around the classroom with a lump in my throat. The Saturday school students have all gone to read the midday prayer before going home. I feel a jolt of happiness when I see that my sticker chart is still hanging behind Sister Sadia's desk. She would add a gold star whenever we finished memorizing a surah—one whole chapter—of the Qur'an, making 114 gold stars in total.

Being back at my old school is making me even more nostalgic. My old desk in front of the classroom has been painted. The doodles I used to scratch onto the surface with my pencil are gone. Why do I keep feeling like I'm being replaced everywhere?

I shake my head. "It sucks."

Sister Sadia perches on her leather chair. "I'm sure there's *something* you like about public school."

I think about it. "Yeah, there's more diversity. And I secretly joined a Muslim boy band." I say that second part quietly.

She laughs, but little does she know. And I don't even know whether Barakah Beats is actually my favorite part of school, or if that's a fib, too. My lies are racking up and it's only been a week. At this rate, I should be turning into Pinocchio. The Nimra at GLA would never have lied and used people the way she is now. But that Nimra never had to fight for Jenna's friendship. That had always been a guarantee.

What a difference a few days can make.

"Have you seen Reema or Hana lately?" I ask her.

"Hana's little sister is in this class, and she comes with her mom to pick her up. It sounds like Hana's liking her new school just fine. I haven't heard from Reema in a while."

"Oh." I'm suddenly very tired and take a seat.

"What's wrong, little tiger?" Sister Sadia's face is open and kind.

I debate telling her about Barakah Beats, but I'm worried that she'll tell my parents. Pretending to be in the band when I'm not committed to it takes so much energy. Still, I can't deny that it was nice spending time with Khadijah and the boys yesterday. They're a fun crew and they're dedicated to doing what they love, even if I don't entirely agree with it. That hidden part of me still makes me feel like a bit of an outcast, though. The whole music thing might not matter to them, but it matters to *me*. What would they think about me if they knew what my real opinion was? Would they understand?

I sigh. "Change is hard."

"It is," Sister Sadia agrees. "Very hard. Be patient, my dear. Once you're settled, I guarantee you won't want to go back to the way things were. It's just natural."

I make a face, and my tongue develops a mind of its own. "Sister Sadia, have you ever lied about something to get what you want? But, like, you had a good reason for it?"

Sister Sadia blinks at me. I feel my neck turn red. "What's a good reason, in your opinion? Sure, I've said things that I wasn't completely honest about before, but I always end up regretting it. Things that begin with dishonesty never end well. Because to tell one lie, you have to tell a hundred."

I'm quiet.

"Is there a reason why you asked me that?"

"No," I lie. I'm sweating the way I used to when I wouldn't practice my Qur'an lessons at home and would come in the next day unprepared to deliver my recitation. Sister Sadia used to see right through me then, and I feel that way now, too.

Thankfully, the Saturday school kids come back from prayer and save me from an interrogation. Families start arriving to pick them up, too.

"Nimra!" Hana squeals when she and her mom show up. We hug and jump up and down like it's been years instead of a few weeks since we last saw each other. Hana and I aren't like best friends, but we still have some fun memories doing Hifz together. "I saw your dad outside! I'm so glad you're here! How's your new school?"

"Fine. What about you?"

Hana sticks her tongue out the side of her mouth and I crack up. "The boys are so *gross*."

"Do you see Reema around? Do you have any classes together?" I ask. I wasn't jealous before about the two girls—who live in the same school district—having a built-in buddy for when they started in public school because I had Jenna's support. At least, I thought I did. But now that jealousy eats me up inside.

Hana grimaces. "Reema hasn't talked to me since school started."

"What? Why?"

"I don't know." Hana looks sad. "She just changed so much, so fast. Reema acts all different now. Sits with the cool kids. She pretends like I don't even exist."

My stomach sinks. It's one thing when non-Muslims do it, but how can another Muslim treat their own like that?

Hana exhales. "But it's okay. I made a friend in Spanish and we hang out sometimes. Still, I wish fitting in wasn't like being in the Olympics."

"Honestly," I mutter.

Hana's mother brings Hana's little sister over by the hand. She pats me on the head and asks about my parents before saying they have to run to make it to a baby shower on time. Hana gives me one last hug. "It was nice seeing you. Don't worry. Things can only get better, right? We just need to have faith."

I used to think it was that easy, too, but middle school isn't called the fifth circle of hell for nothing.

"If you ever want to talk, I'm always here," Sister Sadia says to me after one last goodbye hug. "You know you can tell me anything."

My phone dings on the car ride home. Waleed added me to the Barakah Beats WhatsApp group chat during practice yesterday. Baba's talking to his parents in Pakistan over Bluetooth and doesn't pay attention.

Waleed: What do you guys think of these next lines?

Waleed took what we started on the guitar and is trying to finish the song lyrics while combining them with the keyboard at home. It sounds like a pretty messy way to go about it, but I'm not the expert. With the talent show a month away, Waleed's been acting kinda antsy.

Bilal: I just tried singing them out loud.

Khadijah: Yes, he did. It was awful.

Waleed: Wow, that bad??

Khadijah: No, it's just the way he sounds without autotune.

Bilal: Shut up!!

Waleed: wbu Nimra?

I examine Waleed's lyrics, trying to tune out Dadi's voice in the background as she asks Baba when he's going back to his engineering job (he's not).

Me: It's hard to decide without the music. I like it, though.

Waleed: OK, when I'm done I'll send you guys an instrumental sample.

Bilal: One thing at a time, bro.

Waleed: We gotta get this done. Where's Mattie?

Bilal: Idk. We're at Costco.

Khadijah: Bilal needs glasses.

Bilal: No I don't! That doctor was lying. Khadijah should get them. She's always reading.

Khadijah: Means I'm smart. I can see fine.

I giggle at their exchange. It makes me wish I had a sibling, too.

Matthew: Sorry, guys. I was helping my dad build the crib.

Me: Your mom's having a baby?!

Matthew: She already did . . . over the summer :)

Matthew sends a picture of an adorable pink-cheeked baby chewing her fist. She has her big brother's brown eyes.

Matthew: Her name's Zoya.

Bilal: We know that.

Matthew: I was telling Nimra, smart one.

Khadijah: :D

Waleed: Guys, I'm really nervous about the talent show. Can we focus on that?

Matthew: You've been talking about it so much that I dreamt about it last night.

Waleed: . . . did we win?

Matthew: -__- Dude. I'll work on the acoustics if you just relax.

Waleed: Thanks. Gotta go. I'll keep you guys updated.

Bilal: Sure you will. This week's gonna be fun.

Chuckling, I close out of WhatsApp and pull up my text thread with Jenna.

Me: Hey! Let's go see that new live-action Disney movie tonight. I'm craving a milkshake 😊

Our favorite theater is a fancy dine-in place with this incredible menu. Their salted caramel milkshakes are to die for. Our parents have gotten mad at us before for spending too much on their credit cards. Worth it.

> **Jenna:** 😋 MMMMM milkshakes. Me want. But I can't. We have a team sleepover tonight. You go hang out with your celebrity pals 🙂

Frustration squeezes my brain. I would like to have *one* conversation with Jenna that doesn't involve her bringing up Barakah Beats. Honestly, it's like her new superpower.

> **Me:** What about game night at your place tomorrow?
>
> **Jenna:** Sorry, can't do. We're going to my cousin's birthday party in Maryland. My aunt's taking us to this fancy spa to get our nails done.

I wait for her to suggest another time on her own, but the message never comes. Feeling low, I put my phone away to catch the end of what Baba's saying to Dadi. "Ummi," he sighs. "For the last time, I don't need to go back. The business is doing great. We should have a warehouse secured by the end of next week and we've already started posting jobs online."

"Finally," I say, and cover my mouth.

"Is that Nimra?" Dadi asks loudly in Urdu. "Is she practicing her Qur'an every day? Don't let all her hard work go to waste, Saim!"

"Acha, Ummi, we're almost home. In shaa Allah, I'll talk to you later. Give everyone my salaam." Baba disconnects the call and exhales in relief. He gives me a sympathetic look. "Parents, am I right?"

"Does Mama know you're planning to go to Pakistan in December?"

Baba groans. "You heard that part? I thought you were too busy texting. Who were you talking to, by the way?"

"Jenna. And this other girl named Khadijah at school." It's not a complete lie if I don't mention the other three people.

"You made a new friend." Baba brightens. "That's great. And yeah, maybe I'll go. Don't tell Mama yet. I'm actually trying to set up a tour of northern Pakistan for our anniversary. She's always wanted to visit there. We just never got the chance." Baba can be so romantic.

"That's gonna cost you," I say, poking his arm.

"How much, boss?"

"Krispy Kreme will do."

Baba's evil smile matches mine as he makes a U-turn.

14

On Monday morning, Jenna appears at my locker and puts her arms around me. "Oh my gosh, it's Nimra Sharif! Can I get your autograph? I'm such a huge fan!"

I roll my eyes, rounding on Jenna with my hands on my hips. "Why did you take off without me this morning?" I demand.

"I didn't. Evelyn and I had tryouts before school."

"I waited for you. You couldn't have texted me back?"

"I forgot, Nimra. Jeez. What's gotten into you?" says Jenna.

I hyperfocus on her sleek ponytail all the way down to her newly manicured nails to calm down. Why does she always have to look so perfect?

"Nimra! Hello, hey." Jenna waves her hand in front of my face. "I asked you a question. You've been acting all weird since you started hanging out with Barakah Beats. Do you think you're too cool to hang out with me now because you're friends with a bunch of eighth graders?"

I want to laugh in her face. The obvious jealousy in Jenna's eyes is so rewarding after she foiled all my attempts to meet up this past weekend. "Would you chill out?" I throw her own words back at her. "I think tryout nerves are getting to you. Besides, you're the one whose schedule's packed."

"Oh, stop. I already had plans when you asked me to hang out, otherwise my schedule's not *that* bad."

"Okay. Then how about this Friday after school?" I ask.

Jenna puffs out her cheeks like they're stuffed with marbles. "Actually—"

"Yo, Jenna." Val appears beside us with a wrinkled piece of paper in her hands. She gives me a friendly "Hey, Nimra" before directing all her attention to Jenna. "Did you study for our vocab quiz today?"

"Yup. Quick, use *derogatory* in a sentence. Go!" Jenna challenges her.

"Wait, I know this. Uh. The other team made derogatory comments when we annihilated them in the game. Bam! Two for one!" Val exclaims.

What's derogatory is that my best friend isn't making any time for me outside school. I swing my locker door back and forth as Jenna and Val take turns quizzing each other like I'm not there.

My gaze lands on the digital clock in dismay. "I have to go. My class is in House C. See you later?" I ask hopefully.

"Yep. See you," Jenna says.

I watch her go with Val, disappointed with how that whole thing went.

* * *

Khadijah tracks me down as I'm heading for the cafeteria. She's clutching a new book in one hand. "Are you famous yet?" she teases.

I blush. "No." My gaze slides in the direction of Jenna and her friends. It doesn't feel right to bail on Khadijah right away, so I set my lunch box down at her usual table. But then I remember how she always seems to prefer eating alone and jump back up.

"Where are you going?" asks Khadijah.

"No, um, sorry. I don't want to distract you."

"Wait." Khadijah holds up her hands to stop me. "You can sit with me. If you want. I'm not liking this book anyway." She zips up the book inside her lunch box and unwraps a PB&J sandwich.

I sit down across from her hesitantly. Other than band practice on A days, I only see her in social studies, where Mr. Myer's students get in trouble if he catches them talking about anything that isn't class-related.

I pull my food out of my lunch box. Khadijah beams. "Wow, that looks so good."

"Want some?" I pass her the container of kabob and chicken boti.

Khadijah helps herself and moans into her hands. "*So good.*"

"Thanks. It's my grandma's recipe."

"Do you have a lot of family here?"

I nod. "All of my mom's. My dad's family is in Pakistan. They visit sometimes. What about you?"

"Michigan and Somalia. We're the only ones out here in Virginia," says Khadijah. She chews her food slowly and quietly. Sunnah style, I realize. The way Prophet Muhammad, peace and blessings be upon him, taught us. "It gets pretty boring. I mean, I like it here and the Muslim community is great, but it's not the same. I miss my cousins. Bilal and I always look forward to seeing them over breaks."

"Sometimes family can be a real pain in the butt. Maybe it's a good thing yours is so far away." *Way to sound ungrateful, Nimra.*

Surprisingly, Khadijah smiles. "Oh, I know. I read the most books over the summer."

I choke on a piece of kabob. Khadijah hurriedly passes me a water bottle and I gulp it down. "You said you miss them!" I laugh.

"I do! But they can still be annoying and then I have to do something else." Khadijah shrugs in an it-is-what-it-is way.

"Agreed. What do you like to read?"

"Mostly fiction. I like contemporaries the best. Fantasy, too, if there's dragons," Khadijah says with a gleam in her eyes. "You?"

"The last book I read for fun was in third grade," I

admit. "Actually, I take that back. I started graphic novels last year. They're great. And picture books."

Khadijah lowers her sandwich. "Picture books? Aren't those for little kids?"

"Yeah, but I like looking at the illustrations," I say, unfazed. "I want to do something like that when I'm older. Maybe create my own superhero that everyone wants to cosplay. Oh, or work in animations! That would be the coolest."

"I didn't know you liked art."

"It's just a hobby right now," I say timidly. "But I want to do more with it."

"Wait, so you don't want to be a singer?" Khadijah asks.

My smile turns into a frown. "What made you think that?"

Khadijah shrugs. "You're good at it. And you seem to really enjoy working with the band. Oh, is it because your parents don't take it seriously?"

Uh-oh. "Do yours?" I ask, trying not to sound too suspicious. "I mean, they know about Bilal and Barakah Beats and all that, right?"

"Of course. Matthew and Waleed practically live with us."

For some reason, the idea of the four of them spending time together without me makes me nauseous. "And do they—like it? Your parents, I mean."

"They think the whole band thing is *cute*. They're excited about Barakah Beats performing at the fundraiser, though. They came to the US as refugees, so it means a lot to them. Matthew's parents take it a lot more seriously. His dad's the one who taught him how to play guitar."

Awesome. If—no, *when*—I back out, even their parents will find out what a horrible person I am.

"Just wait till the audience hears you and Bilal together. I'm going to help spread the word because we want as many people to be there as possible. I have some ideas. Waleed put me in charge of the band's social media accounts. Do you think you can hand out flyers at your old school, too?"

My stomach drops. "Wait, how many people are supposed to come to this thing anyway?"

Khadijah shrugs and looks up at the ceiling as if in deep thought. "Hundreds? ADAMS is a pretty big community."

The lunchroom disappears.

"Nimra? Are you okay?"

I gulp before responding. "Uh-huh."

"Should we go pray now?" asks Khadijah. "Are you done?"

I'm more than done. I'm *so* dead. "You go on. I'm on my period, so I can't pray for a few more d—"

"Excuse me."

I jump when Julie appears next to our table. At first I think she must be lost, but she's looking right at me.

"I'd like to talk to Nimra, if you don't mind," Julie says to Khadijah.

Khadijah clamps up even though she was talkative just a minute ago. She gives Julie a sideways glance before shrugging at me and quietly walking off.

"That wasn't nice," I say.

"You keep saying that about me."

"What do you want?" I ask, getting annoyed.

"Jenna thinks you won't sit with us because of me. She's forcing me to apologize for being mean to you," Julie says. She looks pained.

I have to keep my eagerness in check. The funny thing is me eating with Khadijah had nothing to do with avoiding Julie, but Jenna thinking that it did and forcing Julie to come over here to make nice has gotta count for something.

Julie squirms, waiting for me to speak.

"Well?" she prods. "Aren't you going to say something?"

I cross my arms. "I will when you actually apologize."

Julie does not look cool with that answer. "I'm sorry for stereotyping you and for saying that you're not a real artist," she says. "Can we start over?" She sticks out her hand, putting on a desperate look.

I hesitate before shaking her hand. As far as apologies go, that was terrible.

"Will you sit with us now?" Julie asks me.

I nod. "Okay. But I want Khadijah there, too. I don't want to leave her alone."

Julie already knows this is a losing battle. "Fine. She can sit wherever she wants." She pivots and starts walking like she can't get away fast enough. "It's not like the cafeteria has reserved seating or anything."

I'm too psyched to wait until next time. Even though there are only a few minutes left until the bell, I take my stuff and follow Julie over to their table.

"Hey!" Jenna exclaims. There's a light in her eyes that hasn't been there for me in days. It makes my heart twinge happily. "Are we good?" Jenna stares between Julie and me.

"Good enough," Julie says dryly. I could start a fight with her, but I don't want to spoil this moment. Ignoring Julie, I squeeze in beside Jenna and Val on the bench.

"No band practice today?" Evelyn asks, resting her elbows on the table.

"Nope. We only meet on A days," I say, taking all of Jenna's green and yellow Skittles. She hates them, so I don't even have to ask.

"When do we get to hear you in a song?" says Val. "Jenna won't stop bragging about how good your voice is."

My forehead wrinkles. I'm pretty sure Jenna's never even heard me sing.

"I'm trying to hype you up," Jenna whispers in my ear. "You know, for publicity. That way, I can take some of the credit when you're famous." I flick her shoulder playfully.

"We're working on something new right now," I explain. "For a talent show at the mosque in a few weeks. It's to raise money for refugees."

"But that's so far away!" Jenna whines. "I still think you should break out in song at school."

"Yes!" Evelyn exclaims. "Bust it out in here!" She makes a show of standing up on the bench, but Julie yanks her back down.

"I'll get in trouble with Principal Coggins." Luckily, that's a real excuse and they know it.

"You can run, but you can't hide, pal," Jenna says with a straight face. "I'll find a way to break you."

"Good luck with that," I laugh.

"I know you. Remember when you used to be afraid of dogs and I got you to pet our neighbor's dachshund?"

"I did not pet him! He wiggled out of your arms and ran after me!" I was too scared to go to the park after that for a whole week.

Jenna puts her finger on her chin. "Wait, you're right. Oh man, I remember now. It even chased you up the slide." She laughs. "But I saved you!"

"Yeah, right before it attacked my face," I say. It's funny when I think about it now, but it definitely wasn't funny when I was eight and running for my life.

Jenna flips her hair proudly. "Anyway, the point is, I'm

always here to give you a push." She pokes my shoulder for emphasis. "Even when you don't ask for it."

I scoff, but Jenna's comment soothes my worries. Last week, I couldn't shake the feeling that my best friend had been snatched by aliens and replaced by a stranger. Whatever had taken hold of her seems to be gone. This is how it should have been since the first day. It's useless to wish, though. Even if I don't know what that was all about, it's amazing how much better I feel today.

When the bell rings, Jenna pulls me in with her and Julie to walk to PE. I'm floating on cloud nine the whole way.

15

"Right, folks. You're in luck, 'cause it's too hot to run out on the track today," Mr. Peters says, pacing in front of us with his clipboard. Several people make relieved sounds. I fan my face, already warm in my hijab and sweatpants and all we've done so far is warm-up stretches. Today, the seventh and eighth graders are standing shoulder to shoulder against one wall of the main gym. The sixth graders are taking some health class in the other gym.

"Free day!" someone to my left shouts.

"Nice try," Ms. O'Reilly, the eighth-grade PE teacher, says. "You're not off the hook. We're going to treat you to something even better—fitness stations." She waves her arms around, indicating the different equipment set up around the basketball court. Jump ropes, Hula-Hoops, mats. Some of the stations have signs with names of specific workouts on them.

"You get five minutes at each station to do the activity. Think of it like exercise speed dating. You will rotate with your group when you hear the whistle. No standing around. Mr. Peters and I are watching."

We get numbered off and I regret standing next to Jenna when we're split up. Instead, I go over to station ten—the jump ropes—and am greeted by Bilal and Matthew.

"Coincidence," I say.

"Not really. We did these stations last year," Bilal says smugly. "Mattie and I purposely counted how many people were between us. It's only a coincidence you're with us, too!"

A red-haired seventh-grade girl I don't know very well joins our group. Her eyes quietly drift over the three of us in awe. Once everyone is grouped, Mr. Peters goes over to station one—labeled DANCE—where a speaker is set on the floor and pulls out his phone to scroll over the screen while Ms. O'Reilly goes over the rules one last time.

"*Psst*, Nimra." I turn around to face Jenna at station nine. She points at Bilal and Matthew, then at me. "Dance number!" she whisper-yells.

I shake my head vehemently. Jenna plants her fists on her hips.

Her reply is cut off by the music starting. "Five minutes starts—now!" Ms. O'Reilly brings her hand down in an arc.

Matthew tosses me a set of jump ropes. I spend ten seconds disentangling it while the rest of my group starts skipping. The redheaded girl shows off by scissoring her arms.

"What. Is. This. Song?" Bilal complains between jumps. "It. Hurts. My. Ears."

The song Mr. Peters chose isn't—how should I say—*current*. The music sounds stuffy and the lyrics are really cheesy. Several other students make faces at the song choice. Mr. Peters ignores us, gleefully tapping his foot along to the rhythm. My swings become ever lazier.

When five minutes are up, Ms. O'Reilly toots her whistle and we rotate to the next station. Mr. Peters continues his Jurassic playlist.

"Good night, friends," Bilal says, lying down on the mat we're supposed to do push-ups on. "Wake me up when we're listening to something from this century."

Matthew nudges Bilal's stomach with his foot. "Look alive. O'Reilly's coming."

"Let's see if your upper body strength is as good as your lungs," Ms. O'Reilly says, smiling despite her stern expression.

Bilal rolls over on the mat and looks up at her curiously. "You've heard of our band?"

"Heard of you, but never any of your songs. I still bet they're better than this." Ms. O'Reilly points over her shoulder at Mr. Peters swaying his head to the music with his eyes closed. He really is a geezer. The group at station one looks ready to jump him. "This is decades before even my time."

Suddenly, there's silence, except for the squeaking of sneakers and small conversation. We all turn to look at station one. The kids over there look innocent, but I notice one of the boys quickly removing his finger from the speaker. Mr. Peters looks down at his phone and puts it to his ear, dumbfounded.

"Heroes," praises Matthew.

I expect Ms. O'Reilly to go over there and scold them, but she just shrugs. "Oh no," she says sarcastically. She nods at us with green eyes glinting. "What are we going to do now?"

I'm slow to catch on, but Bilal and Matthew jump to their feet, excitement written all over their faces.

No. Ms. O'Reilly can't really mean—

Bilal starts humming and snapping his fingers.

RED ALERT, my mind screams at me. HIDE!

There's no time to make a run for it before the entire class's attention is on our group. Matthew air plays the guitar, imitating realistic sounds with his mouth. Bilal breaks into song—one of Barakah Beats's most popular and upbeat ones—his voice carrying loudly in the gym's open space. Everyone is buzzing now. I locate the exit, ready to fake a period emergency before—

They're surrounding me now. I turn into a statue as

Matthew tosses his hair while going at his invisible guitar. Bilal dances next to me, signaling with his hand for me to join in. Every part of me resists. I can't do anything but stand still, put on the spot, torn between my beliefs and giving in. Bilal's grin slides as he tries to figure me out.

Our classmates don't have the same problem. They clap along, some people even chiming in. I catch Jenna's eye. She swings her hands around like she's having the time of her life. Then she cups her hands around her mouth and yells, "Go, Nimra!"

And it's like time stops. All my hesitation gets shoved to the side as the uncontrollable urge to please her takes over.

I open my mouth, but only a small sound comes out. Reading the look on my face, Bilal stops. He waves the class to be quiet. I wither under everyone's intense gaze. Bilal says something to Matthew and they both face me, blocking my view of the other students. It's like it's just us, like we're in the band room practicing and there's no one to judge us. They start the song over. Bilal and Matthew sing slower this time, eyes locked on me. Giving me courage.

It works. Instinctively, my voice picks up the lyrics. In the background, the clapping resumes. Jenna nods her head supportively. Her reaction and the boys' encouragement spark something inside me. I can't describe what happens next. I sing louder, more confidently, matching Bilal's tempo.

Then there's actual music to the Barakah Beats song. The rebels at station one give us a thumbs-up, Mr. Peters's phone in their hands as our poor teacher scratches his head.

It's like an adrenaline shot through the room. Side by side, Bilal, Matthew, and I go around the gym, pausing in front of each group to bask in the fun with them. Everyone dances to the beat of the music, singing. I wiggle my shoulders a little. At this point, we've all forgotten what we're really supposed to be doing. Even Ms. O'Reilly participates.

Jenna grabs my hand when we reach her group and spins me in a circle. She puts her arms around my waist and bops her head, blonde hair flying. "That's what I'm talking about!" she cheers. "Woo! I knew it. Didn't I tell you?"

It feels like a dream. I look around the room at my classmates—even Julie—having a blast. All my worries melt away in this moment. My best friend is jamming out next to me and PE is basically canceled. Thanks to Barakah Beats.

Best. Class. Ever.

16

"I can't believe I wasn't there!" Waleed says the next day at practice.

Word traveled fast about what went down in eighth-block PE. It's all anyone can talk about. I'm getting recognized now in the hallways and it's overwhelming. Bilal, Matthew, and I spent a few minutes at the beginning of lunch giving Waleed and Khadijah the details.

"Nimra was the GOAT," Bilal says, tipping his chair back into the wall.

"Did you just call me a goat?" I ask, unsure if it's supposed to be a compliment.

"Not 'goat.' GOAT," says Matthew. "You know, like, Greatest Of All Time. You've never heard that before?"

"Uh, no." I mentally add it to my growing list of slang words. There are so many I've never heard of before. I feel silly when even my teachers understand what it all means and I don't.

"Really? Are you online? I can't find you anywhere," Waleed says. "I thought maybe you keep all your profiles private."

"Nope. I don't have any."

"None? At all?" Matthew asks in surprise.

"Never. I just got a phone before school started."

Khadijah gapes at me. "So, where do you post your artwork? You said you draw, right?"

I pop a halal gummy bear in my mouth, chewing slowly. "I don't share my stuff on the Internet," I finally confess. "Or with anyone."

"If you want to do all the things you said you wanted, then you kind of have to share your work with other people," Khadijah says.

"Yeah, fight those fears. Like you did yesterday," Bilal

adds helpfully. "We totally believe in you. Start small. You know, get at least one account like a normal person."

I wrap the end of my hijab around my finger. "I don't know."

"It's easy. Here. Give me your phone," says Waleed. I do, but only because I don't have an excuse. Waleed downloads a photo-sharing app and has me create an account. Then he shows me how to add all four of them, plus Barakah Beats's official account, to my followers list.

"There. Now you can upload all you want. Post one of your pictures when you get home and tag all of us." I doubt I'll do that, but I nod anyway. Before I forget, I quickly search up Jenna and send her a request, too.

"Wow, Nimra. Music *and* art? How did we get so lucky?" asks Bilal. "You're going to take over the world."

I bite my lips. It was nice having Jenna fangirl all over me on the way home from school yesterday—we even had a snack together before she went home. It was like the old days. While the impromptu dance session in PE was more fun than I want to admit, it did create a little problem. It made my place in the band even more public and set off the wagging finger in my mind. The one that likes to remind me that underneath all the laughs, nothing can erase the guilt I feel inside. The harder I try to justify to myself why I'm still in the band, the more I feel bad about hiding who I am and the type of Muslim I'm comfortable being.

Now I think I might've taken it too far. My plan to win Jenna is working better than ever. There's no point in me sticking around anymore and keeping up this charade or risking my secret getting out to my parents.

And yet, I can't seem to tell that to the boys.

It *shouldn't* be hard. It's only been one week since I agreed to join the band. I should be able to make up some excuse and walk right out of here without looking back.

Then I imagine coming to school and never hearing Waleed's excitement and worry again, or seeing Matthew rolling his eyes, or laughing at Bilal's jokes. And how would I face Khadijah in social studies for the rest of the year if I back out? Even if there's a teeny tiny chance she'll understand and we can still be friends, she might never trust me again.

I'm stuck. If I leave Barakah Beats, I leave all of it.

Good going, Nimra! I kick the chair in front of me in frustration.

"Whoa, what's up?" asks Matthew.

"Nothing. My foot fell asleep." LIES. "Let's just work on this." We've been ironing out the lyrics and refining our vocal melodies and how it's all going to come together in the chorus.

"Nimra, those were the wrong lyrics. And you're sort of off-key," Khadijah comments after our first run-through. *Then do me a favor and kick me out.* Instead, she shows me a you-got-this attitude and has me start over.

"Guys, I'm sorry. I'm just not feeling it today," I say after the fourth time I mess up.

"You get a pass," Bilal says cheerily. "I know. Why don't you read something from the Qur'an? It might help clear your head."

"I usually have them freestyle when they're stuck," says Khadijah. She gives Bilal a look of sisterly annoyance. "But that's a good idea, too. And I've never heard you recite before."

I can actually use the distraction. I clear my throat, thinking about Surah An-Nasr, one of the shorter and easier chapters. Several seconds pass. Then a minute.

Then another minute. It isn't until the four of them are looking at me strangely that I realize what's happening.

I've blanked.

"Wait. I know this. It's—"

Try as I might, I can't remember how to start the surah. My cheeks flame as panic grips me. I squeeze my head between my hands. *Come on, what is it?*

"It's okay, Nimra," Khadijah says, putting her hand on my shoulder. "You're just tired. It's not a big deal. We all forget sometimes."

Not me! I want to shout at her. *I'm a hafiza.*

Lying is turning me into a hot mess. That's the only explanation. The shame that never leaves the back of my mind every time I get together with Barakah Beats is doing this. Sketching has never done this to me before. With art, I don't have to think about whether what I'm doing is right or wrong.

My eyes sting with embarrassment. Waleed mouths something I can't hear. A minute later, I realize he isn't *saying* anything to me. He's reciting Ayatul Kursi, one of the most famous and memorized passages from the

Qur'an. His voice mixed with the Arabic is so musical. Like a ballad. All I can do is stare. Halfway through, Bilal and Matthew harmonize with Waleed. They read and tap their feet with the same passion as one of their songs. When they reach the end, they start over. To my surprise, Khadijah tunes in this time. She's shy about it, but I pick out bits of her voice from the boys'. She sounds good! Her voice is nowhere near as bad as she keeps saying it is.

I realize what they're trying to do. My mind charges up and Ayatul Kursi bursts from my tongue. Waleed's eyes dance at my comeback. Not wanting to lose steam, I transition back into our song for the talent show. This time, I run through the entire thing without a single mistake. Best of all, Bilal and I aren't alone this time. Waleed, Matthew, and Khadijah sing along from memory, too.

Something about this moment makes all the cells in my body light up. I don't want it to end. I want to soak up every little sound and save it somewhere special in my brain to come back to whenever I want. I've never felt a connection like this to anything except my art.

I go overboard when we finish and nearly knock Khadijah out of her chair in excitement. "You liar! You *can* sing! Did you guys hear that? Did you hear us?" I squeal. "Why is it just Bilal and me singing for the show? The five of us should sing as a group!"

Khadijah shakes her head and scoots away. "No way, Jose."

"Why not?"

"I only did that to help jog your memory," says Khadijah. She drags an imaginary zipper across her lips. "My job here is done."

I smirk. "What if I keep forgetting?"

"You better not!" Khadijah says in a bossy voice. "I'm not doing that again."

I start singing horribly on purpose to mess with her. The boys cringe and cover their ears.

"You're fired." Khadijah laughs.

"Okay, I think that little exercise worked," Matthew says kindly. "Good job, everyone. By next week, we should be doing more fine-tuning."

I unlock my phone screen in shock. "We're out of time already?"

"Yeah, the bell's about to ring," Waleed says.

"Wait. No one else likes my idea about us singing together?" I ask.

"That's not how the song's written, Nimz. Every track has its main players. We're the stars of this one," Bilal explains loftily. "The others are just background."

Matthew jabs Bilal with his guitar. "We're still important."

"Of course you are," Bilal coos. He narrowly avoids another dig to his side.

"Mattie and I have to focus on playing the keyboard and guitar," Waleed says.

"I guess," I concede.

Khadijah makes an announcement before the room clears out. "Next time, we're going to talk about T-shirt designs. Bring your ideas!"

When Khadijah and I are the only ones left in the band room, I turn to her. "T-shirts?"

"Yup. I want to design us matching costumes for the show. We're a group, so we should look it. Do you want to help me?" Khadijah asks hopefully. "You're probably a lot better at drawing than I am."

"Sure." I try to sound casual and not like I'm dying to take it over. I might even start a rough sketch next block in Spanish instead of zoning out. I hate that class only because I could've been in art if my parents had let me take it. I get sad when I see other students' artwork displayed in the hallway. Maybe someone would've looked at my picture hanging on the wall and thought, *Wow, that one's awesome.* Guess I'll never know.

Or will I? I swipe my phone on and navigate to my new profile. A blank wall just for me. I force myself to close out of it but go to Spanish more distracted than usual.

17

I've always been proud of every single one of my sketches no matter what. I didn't care if it took me a few minutes or a few days to make. Nothing beats the feeling of bringing my imagination to life.

Thanks to social media, now I know they actually suck.

The search bar is my new nemesis. There are hundreds of accounts full of some of the most amazing artwork I've ever seen. Each one is like a mini punch to the gut when I compare it with my own.

I'm in over my head, I think, buried underneath a blanket on the basement sofa on Saturday afternoon. The current page I'm stalking has over a thousand followers with realer-than-life dot art. *I'll never be this talented.* If

Waleed and the others saw these, they would tell me to delete my profile.

My profile page is still emptier than Mr. Myer's heart. It feels wrong to put so much time into music when it is only stirring up guilt inside me, and all the while I'm doing nothing with my art even though that's what I actually want to do. Well, that's not going so well either.

I throw my phone with its in-your-face-beautiful pictures on the carpet just as the basement lights blind me. Squealing, I yank the blanket over my face.

"Why are you lying here in the dark?" asks Mama, standing in the middle of the room in black tights and a long T-shirt. "Don't you— Oh, wow. What's all this?" She stares at the dozens of half-finished sketches strewn all over the floor.

"My failures," I say glumly. I went into a frenzy today trying to prove to myself I'm not an amateur. That I can draw something good enough that other people can admire. Big nope.

Doodling for fun doesn't count. Maybe Julie was right. Maybe I'm not cut out for this.

Mama whistles. "You sure worked up a sweat today.

I like this one." She picks up a crumpled page with a sad attempt at a hijabi superhero.

"Mama, a five-year-old can draw better than that," I say irritably. "Turn the lights off, please. I'm sulking."

She slings the comforter back. "Well, come sulk with me upstairs. Baba's out running errands and I'm bored of processing orders. You hungry?"

"No, thanks."

The corners of Mama's eyes crinkle. "I brought Halal Guys."

"On second thought, I'm starving."

Mama sets out two platters in the kitchen and saves the third for Baba. We take our food to the table, digging in silently. I tie my long hair back so it doesn't get in my mouth.

"Where's Jenna nowadays?" Mama says, spearing a chicken covered in white sauce. "She doesn't come by as much anymore."

"Oh, volleyball's taking over her life. I see her at school, though." The second half of B days are awesome because I get to hang out with Jenna from lunch until the end of

PE. Khadijah never comes to our table, even though I've been asking her to all week. She assures me she's fine and sits alone, reading at her usual spot. I only sat with her that one time, but it still feels wrong to bail on her. Even though I see Khadijah in first block and band practice on A days, I miss her during B-day lunch.

"How's school?" Mama asks abruptly. "Is it getting any better?"

I swallow a forkful of spicy rice. "Yeah. It's pretty good. I hang out with some, um, kids in my class. They're nice."

"Honey, that's great. I'm so happy you're putting yourself out there."

I set my fork down. I can't talk to her about Barakah Beats, but I can talk to her about art. "Mama, do you think my drawings are any good?"

Mama brushes a piece of hair—dark brown in the sunlight shining through the sliding deck doors—off her face and looks at me, surprised. "Nimra, your drawings are some of the best I've ever seen for someone your age."

I wilt. "Someone my age?"

"Creativity blooms with experience. You've only been sketching for, what, four years?"

"Seven! I should've gotten somewhere by now. Do you know how many artists have their own webcomics and studios and fans who look forward to seeing their next project?"

"Slow down. What are you talking about?"

"Look!" I flip my phone screen over with the app still open for her eyes to feast on. "Some of these people aren't even that much older than me."

Mama stares quietly. "When did you get social media?"

"A few days ago. Mama, focus!" I say, pressing my phone to her face. "See how many followers they have?"

"It's not a race, Nimmy. Do you think that happened to them overnight? Don't compare yourself to others. Everyone has to start somewhere. You won't even let me put your work on the fridge."

"Guess I always knew it wasn't good enough," I grumble, sitting back in my chair. "Or maybe I would be better if you had let me take art instead of Spanish."

Mama blinks. "Why do you have to take art at school? You're always drawing and improving on your own. Why can't you do this one thing for us? Knowing Spanish is a great skill."

"I could learn Spanish on my own, too! I want a real art teacher there to tell me what I'm doing wrong. Otherwise, I can't keep getting better. You and Baba don't get it. You don't understand how much it means to me." I sit there stewing, forcing back tears.

Mama purses her lips, thinking. "Actually, we do understand."

"Sure doesn't seem like it!" I throw my hands up in the air, so wound up I forget to watch my tone. Mama gives me a hard look but ignores it.

"Let me show you something. I'll be right back." Mama stands up and leaves the kitchen. Her footsteps pad up the stairs and I hear her bedroom door open. A few minutes later, she reappears with an old square shoebox. Mama brings it to the table and lifts the lid. I gasp.

Inside are my old drawings, including the first picture I ever drew since I started calling myself an "artist." It's an image of myself . . . drawing. Real original. Picture-me is sitting at a desk with a dream bubble coming out of her head, imagining herself grown up with a mighty pencil.

My lines aren't solid, and my shading is, well, bad. Still, it's not the worst considering I drew it when I was seven.

"You kept these?" I ask Mama, digging through the box's contents. Folded napkins, lined paper, printer paper, and even a barf bag from a plane on a trip to Pakistan. A shock of pink catches my eye and, amazingly, I uncover my first sketchbook. I was so sure I'd thrown it away.

"Baba gave this to you when you completed your first fast for Ramadan. You were eight," Mama says over my shoulder. "You filled it up in a month. See how much you've improved in that span of time?"

"That was the year I started Hifz," I say, sliding a hand over the soft cover. "I was so nervous. I didn't think I could do it. I used to draw every night before bed because it calmed me down. Sometimes I drew and memorized at the same time."

"I used to stop you, remember?" Mama says. "I wanted you to give the Qur'an your full attention when you were spending time with it. But it was obvious that drawing helped you memorize better, so I let it go." Mama looks down at me with a knowing smile. "How could I not know how important art is to you after that? The problem isn't that you're not a good artist, or that you need a teacher. I know it's nice to have a mentor, but you're not giving yourself enough credit, Nimmy. You have so much confidence with the Qur'an, but you're always hiding your art. You have to be brave enough to share what you love."

"Like a tiger," I say. "They're brave."

"That's right." Mama taps me on the nose. "If you always second-guess yourself, then you'll never grow to where you want to be. And don't worry about what other people are going to think. Art should make you happy, whether it makes you famous or not."

I look down at the shoebox full of hopeful little Nimra's drawings. "So, you think it's worth a shot?"

"It doesn't have to be today. Whenever you're ready," says Mama. "I have to get back to work. Can you put these back in the box?"

"Mama?" I say before I lose my nerve. She just told me to be brave, and that's what I'm doing. Brave people don't lie. They don't fake who they are or pretend to agree with something they don't. For a tiny second, I want to tell her everything about the band and the talent show. But I scrap the idea. The band, the music, that's not what I want to fight for. I want to be brave for what my heart really wants.

I swallow and say, "I still don't want to take Spanish. I really want to take art at school."

Mama sighs. "I'll discuss it with Baba and see what he thinks."

It's better than nothing.

I take the rest of my food to the basement. I clean up the mess I made and get comfortable on the couch with a sharpened pencil and new page. The blank space sets my mind in motion like magic. I draw the first line down the middle. The picture forms in my head, and I know immediately what's supposed to be there. I silently draw. First comes a face. Then eyes, body, tail. And lastly, stripes, a wispy mane. In the end, a semi-ferocious young tiger stares back at me.

I pick up my tiger napkin sketch, its wise eyes staring back like it's sending me a message. I write "Little Tiger" at the top and sign my name at the bottom. Then I hold it up against the glass doors leading out to the backyard.

The sun creates a cool backlit effect, making the tiger look like it's glowing. I take a picture with my phone and, after choosing a filter with more contrast, post it for my seven followers before I chicken out.

My first like comes from Waleed while I put everything away. He left a comment, too.

A king by the queen herself. ☺ **Keep 'em coming!**

18

We get our first algebra test back less than three weeks before the fundraiser. Waleed comes running into House B the next morning like his sneakers are on fire.

"Holy smokes!" I jump out of the way before we crash.

"I need your help," Waleed says. He falls against the lockers, gasping. Julie does a double take a few rows down. She looks at the two of us, then away, slamming her locker shut and strutting off.

"What happened?" I ask.

"I got a sixty-eight on the algebra test. My parents are really mad and said they would take away my keyboard and computer if I don't bring my grade up. We have that problem set Yariks gave us last class and I don't know how to do any of the problems! Help me, Nimra!" Waleed shakes me by the shoulders. "I can't let that happen!"

"Slow down," I say, pulling out of his grasp. "How did you get a sixty-eight? You're good at math."

"I didn't study for the test," Waleed admits sheepishly. "I was practicing the keyboard part for our song 'cause I want it to sound perfect."

"Waleed! You're obsessed."

Waleed puts his head in his hands and slumps to the ground. "I know! I wasn't thinking! My parents are pissed. They already think music distracts too much from school." He looks up at me. "Can you show me how to do the problem set? You're at lunch when I'm in study hall, right? We can work in the library."

I can't help but feel sympathetic, and a little pleased that he asked me when there are so many other people he could ask. "Okay," I say quietly. "Come to the library during lunch. Bring your problem set."

Waleed scrambles to his feet. "Thank you, thank you. You're saving my life right now. I promise I'll be the best tutee you've ever had."

"Tutee?"

"Tutor." He points at me, then himself. "Tutee."

I give him my best impersonation of a stern math teacher. "All right, Mr. Tutee. Don't forget to bring your calculator." He bows dramatically before darting back to House A.

Jenna appears at my elbow, looking all excited. "What was he doing here?"

"Asking about algebra stuff," I say.

"Nerds. Hey, they just dropped a new trailer for the next Avengers movie. Don't worry, I didn't watch it yet. I'm waiting to watch it with you at lunch."

My insides light up, but then I remember what I just promised Waleed.

"Sorry, I can't eat with you today. I already made plans to help Waleed with homework."

Jenna's face contorts in horror. "OMG, you're going to make me break tradition? I can't believe you're choosing homework over the Avengers! Where's Nimra, you imposter?"

"Just wait until school's over," I say. "We'll watch it while walking home." That way, Evelyn, Val, and Julie won't be there to watch us geek out. I like it to just be Jenna and me. It's our thing.

"No way. I can't wait that long. I'll just make a video of my reaction and send it to you."

That sets off all my alarms. "No, don't! Okay, what if I show up at the beginning of lunch and leave after watching the trailer with you? Waleed won't care if I'm a little late."

"Yay!" Jenna says.

I frown. If our tradition was that important to her, she would wait for me. I would do it for *her.*

"We have to do something after school one day, too," I say. "We haven't *talked* talked in forever."

"I know. I've been getting a lot more homework and then have volleyball on the weekends. Like, literally every weekend." Jenna shrugs. "Maybe when the season's over. I'll let you know."

She waves goodbye, and melts into the crowd. I watch her go, not feeling as happy as I should feel about that plan.

At lunch, I meet Jenna in the cafeteria to watch the trailer with her and then race to the library. Waleed is sitting at one of the square tables near the computers. He waves me over.

"Sorry I'm late," I say. I try to sound like I mean it because I'm still dying from that trailer. Jenna and I gasped out loud at one point.

"It's cool. I got started," says Waleed. He shows me his paper.

"Is that a graph?" I tilt my head upside down. "Why does it have a tail?"

"Because there are, like, three equations for a line and I don't know which one to use," Waleed grumbles. "And she doesn't give us any coordinates, so how am I supposed to solve for slope?"

"You didn't learn this stuff in pre-al?" I ask.

Waleed sits back in his chair and for some reason looks embarrassed. "I didn't take pre-al. I was in Math Seven last year and did really well, so my teacher said that I should skip pre-al and go straight to algebra. My parents wouldn't let me sign up for anything else."

"At least you know how to simplify things," I say, smiling.

He grins back. "I don't know why I don't get it."

"Maybe it has something to do with you falling asleep every class?"

"It's boring!" Waleed says defensively.

I scoff. "Try repeating the same Qur'anic verse over and over for hours until it sounds perfect. Now *that's* boring." I dig through my backpack for my problem set and a pencil and lay them out on the table. "Let me show you a neat trick." I go over last class's lesson in as little time as possible and show him how to draw a graph from an equation and vice versa.

Waleed listens without interrupting. I don't know if anything I'm saying helps until he attempts one of the problems himself. "I think I got it," he says, and shows it to me.

I clap quietly. "Right! Well, I think that's right. That's what I got, too."

"Then it's right." Waleed twirls his pencil between his fingers. "For someone who's artsy, you're really good at math. I bet you're the favorite in art class, too."

I fiddle with my pencil. "I'm not taking art."

"*What?* Why not?"

"I only had one elective and my parents said taking

a language was more practical. So, I'm taking Spanish instead."

Waleed's face falls, like he understands. "Parents suck sometimes."

"But they love how much I love art," I say quickly. "They would never make me stop unless I choose to. They promised to buy me more expensive supplies if I stick to it."

Waleed sighs. "You're lucky. I literally begged my dad for a keyboard."

"How did you get into music?" I ask.

"My cousin in Pakistan started teaching me how to play. He works in the industry over there and has even worked with a few celebrities. I've wanted to be just like him ever since I was little. And then I met Matthew and Bilal. We make a good team." Waleed's brown eyes are thoughtful and bright on me. "I just want us to win this show so badly. I know it makes me a little obnoxious."

"No, it just means you love music," I say. Waleed has a real gift, even if he goes overboard with it sometimes. I wish some of his confidence would rub off on me with my drawings.

"Do you like it here?" Waleed asks suddenly.

The question takes me aback. I fold my arms in front of me on the table and shrug.

Waleed tilts his head. "What does that mean?"

"Sometimes I miss my old school," I confess. "I know it sounds boring. We didn't have a gym or cafeteria or fancy technology or lots of teachers and kids in the program, but GLA was like home to me."

"So then why did you come to public school?" asks Waleed.

"I had to eventually," I reply. "Besides, I only went to GLA for their Hifz program, and I finished it this summer."

Waleed nods. "For what it's worth, I'm glad you transferred. I'm glad that you're here and we got to meet you and that you're part of the band. I can't wait until you finally get to be onstage with us."

I smile weakly and I bet it looks as fake as I feel. Is there ever a good time to reveal to your bandmate that you've been lying to them this whole time? At this point, I think being honest with them is the best way for me to get out of the performance. Things with Jenna are still a bit rocky, but there's just no time for me to come up with something better. Every day that I delay, the inevitable weighs down on me extra hard.

"And think about all the awesome songs we'll write together after the fundraiser," Waleed continues. "It'll be a little harder next year when the three of us go to high school, but we'll figure it out. As long as you're around to tutor me in math, there's no way Papa can get mad."

I bite my pencil. He's thinking *that* far ahead? Oh, the boys and Khadijah are gonna hate me when they find out the truth.

"Your dad seemed nice, though," I say, desperate to change the subject.

"I didn't say he was *mean*. It's just that my brother is studying to be an engineer and he's going to have a good job one day and Papa thinks that I won't. We can prove him wrong, though. We can show him that music can be a real job and it can change lives!"

"You love music that much, huh? It makes you happy."

He nods. "It's who I am."

His words fan the small flame of guilt in my chest. I don't want to be the reason Waleed's dream falls apart.

I shouldn't have kept going to band practice and gotten his hopes up about winning. Now the band's counting on me.

And the truth is . . . part of me still *wants* to sing. There are times I can even ignore the guilty, strict voice inside my head. But then other times, I want to put myself in time-out forever.

This is the *worst*.

Waleed flips the problem set to the next page and works quietly. I look at his face, imagine how disappointed he'll be when I tell him the truth, and I just know.

I can't drop out. I have to sing with Barakah Beats at the ADAMS fundraiser. I don't have a choice.

19

"We only have two weeks left before the fundraiser," Waleed says during Friday practice later that week. He paces the band room anxiously. "Is that enough time? Are we ready?"

"We've got the music down pat," says Matthew, cradling his guitar.

"Nimz and I got this," Bilal says, raising his fist in solidarity. I nod, throwing up a fist of my own.

Khadijah makes an unsure sound and Waleed turns frantically. "What's wrong?"

"It's still missing something," she says. "It's the way the song ends. It doesn't stay with me, you know?"

"What do you mean it's *missing something*?" Waleed

demands. "We've been practicing for *days* and you're just saying this *now?*"

"Way to go, K," Bilal says. "You're going to give him nightmares."

Khadijah holds her hands up apologetically. "I'm just being honest!"

"We need more time," Waleed says. "We should meet over the weekend and practice some more."

"No, we need to *chill*," says Matthew. "We're gonna do *fine*. Even the best artists need a break."

"Yeah, we haven't just hung out in forever," Bilal says. "My throat hurts. I vote for movie night."

Matthew nods. "I'm cool with that."

"Me three!" says Khadijah.

I clench my teeth. I don't know if Mama and Baba will approve of that. They don't like me going out with people they don't know. They'll know right away something's up. But I don't want to be left out of the fun. Unless . . .

An idea pops into my head. "Let's watch at my place! I've got a big-screen TV and lots of snacks."

Matthew looks over at me in surprise. "Really? Your parents will be okay with that?"

"Sure." At least, I *hope* they will be.

Matthew flashes a smile. I can see why Julie has a crush on him. He really *is* cute.

"Awesome. Party in Nimra's crib!" whoops Bilal.

"We have to ask permission first, dum-dum," Khadijah says.

"Like Aabe and Hooyo are gonna care."

Waleed doesn't look convinced it's a good idea. "I don't know, you guys. We still need to practice . . ."

I feel bad about outnumbering him, but it's not my biggest betrayal. "Waleed, they're right. It's just one day. Then we'll focus extra hard until the show."

The fight goes out of him. Finally, Waleed gives in. "Okay."

"Tomorrow evening at my house. I'll text you guys the address," I say.

*   *   *

I tell Mama and Baba I'm having friends over the next day and they switch to super-host mode, which involves a lot of running around, sweeping things off the sofas and tables, and making sure there's room to walk.

"We're going to be in the basement most of the time," I say.

"The house should still be presentable," Mama says, straightening the cushions once more. Boxes have started to move out to the warehouse and what's left gets stacked in storage. I forgot what our house looked like without the clutter.

The next evening, I come downstairs wearing a red floral-printed hijab. Baba raises his eyebrows and grins. "Why have you got that on, Nimmy? Boys coming over?"

I roll my eyes. If anyone is showing off, it's the two of them. They're dressed up today like they're hosting royalty, not a bunch of middle schoolers.

My palms start sweating when the doorbell rings. I dash to open it, but Baba beats me to it, sticking his tongue out. The playfulness comes to a complete halt when he opens the door and is met by Khadijah and the guys.

"Assalamu alaikum," Matthew says happily. The others chorus the greeting. Baba backs away from the door like it's a prank. Guess I *should* have warned him I was having boys over. I thought he'd take the hint when I came downstairs in my hijab.

"Waalaikumusalam." Mama pops in behind us and waves everybody into the tiny foyer. She doesn't even blink as the three boys take their shoes off while smiling at an uncomfortable-looking Baba. "Did your parents already leave?"

"We carpooled," says Khadijah. "Matthew's mom drove us."

"Oh, how nice."

"Mama, Baba," I say. "You already know Waleed. This is Bilal, Khadijah, and Matthew."

"Wonderful to meet you!" exclaims Mama. "Come on in."

"You have a beautiful house," Bilal comments. "Our mom sent this." He hands Mama a foil-covered tray, which she takes with a thank-you.

"This is for you." Waleed holds up a small gift bag to me. "Graphite pencils. I thought you might like them. Don't forget to give me pencil creds on your posts," he jokes. I clutch the bag, surprised by his kindness. Waleed turns to Baba. "Saim Uncle, Papa says salaam."

When Baba doesn't respond, Mama steps on his foot behind the counter. "Waalaikumusalam," he says. "Sorry. Uh, Nimmy, you didn't mention—?"

"We're gonna go downstairs to watch a movie," I announce loudly. "Is that okay?"

"Yeah, I guess . . ." says Baba. Khadijah meets my eyes behind his back and snickers into her shirt.

"I'll bring the snacks in a bit," says Mama. "You kids go ahead."

"Keep the doors—wait, there are no doors. Never mind." Baba makes a shooing gesture and I make a beeline for the stairs with the four of them at my heels.

"At least he didn't faint," Bilal whispers, and we smother our giggles.

We spill into the open room and they take in the decorated suite.

"Whoa. You have your own studio," Waleed says, looking around.

"Only when my grandparents aren't here." I'm happy they think it's cool, and double happy they never had to see Cardboard Land.

Bilal flops down on the couch with his hands behind his head and one socked foot up on the armrest. "I could get used to this. You're so lucky you don't have to share any of this with a sibling." Khadijah smacks him over the head.

"Gah!" Bilal says. "Mattie, have fun while Zoya's still a baby. See how aggressive sisters are?"

"How can you call this innocent face aggressive?" I say with my hands on Khadijah's shoulders. "She's a sweetheart." Khadijah flashes an angelic smile.

Bilal shakes his head. "Try living under the same roof."

Khadijah rolls her eyes. "I'm the one they should feel bad for. Do you know he leaves his dirty laundry around the house? It's so nasty."

"And you always leave your books lying around. What if I trip on one and die?"

"Hey, are all of these yours?" Matthew interrupts, inspecting a stack of notebooks on the floor next to the TV stand. He flips through the sketches and holds up a drawing for the others to see of The Flash (my second favorite superhero after Spider-Man) that I did a few months ago. "Check it out. They look so real. Why aren't you posting any of these?"

"They're not, uh, finished," I say. "I jump around a lot."

I fiddle with my fingers awkwardly as they admire my work. Waleed looks up and locks gazes with me. He cracks a half smile. My face reddens.

"What movie should we watch?" I ask, picking up the remote to change the subject. "I'm allowed to rent almost anything I want."

"No horror," Bilal says immediately. "I can't sleep afterward."

I browse down the menu and land the cursor on a title that catches my eye. "How about *The Greatest Showman*? I've never seen it."

"Me neither," Waleed says.

"I'll watch anything with Zendaya over and over," Bilal says, batting his eyelashes.

"That's how I feel about Tom Holland," I say, then wince. Why did I say that?!

"You have a crush on Tom Holland?" Khadijah grins.

"He's a good Spider-Man!"

"He really is," Matthew agrees.

Mama brings us popcorn and soda as I draw the curtains closed and curl up next to Khadijah. "Baba ordered pizza. It'll be here soon. I grabbed some extra cushions and blankets for you guys, too. Help yourselves. Let me know if there's anything else I can get you." Mama pats me on the head before going back upstairs.

"Your mom's really nice," Khadijah says.

"Is she excited to hear you sing with us?" asks Bilal. "Your parents are coming to the fundraiser, right?"

I bite my lip. "Maybe. If they're not busy."

"I convinced my brother to come home and watch us," Waleed says excitedly. "My cousins will be there, too."

I'm relieved Mama left the room already. I've been trying to come up with a way to tell Mama and Baba about the talent show. Time's running out. How bad would it be if I dragged them to the fundraiser without telling them about the performance? The worst that can happen is I get in a lot of trouble afterward and they never talk to me again, but at least it would be over. I'd just spend the rest of my life thinking about how it ruined my relationship with my parents. I might even have to ask Nano and Nana to move in with them.

Yeah, definitely bad.

The movie starts and the five of us quiet down, but my brain is louder than ever now. I pull the coverlet up to my chin and stare blankly ahead. I've never watched a movie with kids my own age besides Jenna. As much as I love my little cousins, they don't always like to include me.

Here with Waleed, Matthew, Bilal, and Khadijah, I don't have to sit by myself and draw. I've gotten used to it—love it even—but for once, it's not such a bad thing to trade my pencils in for some real friends.

"Bilal, quit hoarding all the popcorn," Matthew complains. "You've literally eaten half the bowl already and Hugh Jackman is still a kid."

"You eat too slow," says Bilal. He stuffs a handful of popcorn in his mouth and chews obnoxiously.

"Share, dude!" Matthew reaches for the bowl and Bilal yanks it out of reach above his head, cackling.

"That's how it's gonna be, huh? Fine. Let's settle this the usual way." Matthew rolls off the couch and stands with his hands on his hips. "I challenge you to . . . a sing-off!"

I stare between them. "A *what*?"

"Sing-off! Sing-off!" chants Khadijah.

"Winner gets extra pizza!" Bilal says, springing to his feet. "What song?"

Matthew rolls his shoulders, looking serious. "'Rewrite the Stars.'"

"But that doesn't come on until later in the movie," says Khadijah.

"Forward it. I get Efron's part."

"Fine. I don't mind being Zendaya," Bilal says, cracking his knuckles. He and Matthew are standing in the middle of the room like they're about to wrestle each other.

"What is going on?" I demand. "Someone needs to explain this to me."

"Don't worry, they do this all the time," Khadijah says. "Just watch."

I let Khadijah take the remote and she fast-forwards to a scene where a sad Zac Efron and Zendaya are standing alone on the circus stage. A dramatic pause fills the room right before Khadijah hits play.

The number starts slow. Matthew copies Zac Efron's movements, circling Bilal and serenading him in a spot-on impression of the character's lovesick voice. As the song picks up, Matthew grabs Bilal by the waist and spins him around slowly, their faces almost touching in a romantic gesture. I giggle, but Khadijah gestures for me to keep watching.

Zendaya's part takes over and Bilal picks up the lyrics.

He dramatically demonstrates her character's acrobatic skills by repeatedly jumping on the sofas and leaping over our laps while singing. When Zac and Zendaya swing around each other in the air, Matthew and Bilal twirl like ballerinas, singing at the top of their lungs.

At last the music crescendos, and as Zac and Zendaya grab on to each other to execute the perfect loop, Matthew and Bilal—too caught up in spinning toward each other—smash heads and fall backward. They lie on the ground, groaning, as the song fades away.

Waleed is the first one to burst out laughing. I hold my stomach as Khadijah and I crack up, too.

"I'd clap, but my hands are full," says a voice on the stairs.

I choke at the sight of Baba holding pizza boxes and paper plates. "That was quite the show," he says.

"Judges?" Khadijah asks. "What's your verdict?"

Waleed gets it together and shakes his head. "It's a no from me," he says.

"Epic fail," I agree.

"That's not fair!" Bilal throws up his hands. Matthew rubs his head with a frown. "My Zendaya was flawless."

Khadijah shrugs. "Sorry. You both lose. No one gets extra pizza."

"Oh, I wouldn't worry about that," Baba says, dropping the pizza box open in front of us. "There's plenty to go around."

"I might have a bruise for nothing," Matthew mutters, rubbing his forehead.

"At least now we know you guys have what it takes to join the circus," Khadijah says. She passes the stack of plates around the circle we make sitting on the floor. I flick my eyes toward Baba, willing him with all my might to go back upstairs. He doesn't move, instead serving pizza to everyone like a good adult.

"That reminds me," Khadijah says. "I finalized our T-shirts for the big day."

I almost drop the slice of cheese pizza Baba's trying to hand me.

"I wanted to get your approval before my mom orders them. Look." Khadijah flips her phone over to show us the image and I gasp. The drawing on the sample T-shirt is the logo I gave to Waleed.

"How did you get that?" I whisper.

"Pretty cool, right? Waleed sent me a picture of it. Nothing else came close to it. I'm going to need everyone's size and then I'll have them printed."

Baba stares at the picture. "That looks like Nimmy's handiwork." He squints closer at the screen. "What's this for? And what's Barakah Beats?"

The question drops like a bomb in the middle of a peaceful sanctuary. Waleed, Matthew, Bilal, and Khadijah glance at Baba with their eyebrows squished together. My mouth dries like it's been stuffed full of sand.

Waleed lowers his pizza and grimaces. "Barakah Beats is—" he says uncertainly, and stops. "Wait, you don't—"

The look in Waleed's eyes shocks my voice awake. "Baba, you forgot the soda. And napkins. My hands are already greasy."

"Whoops. I'll get 'em," says Baba, and thank God, he finally leaves.

"What was that?" Matthew asks the minute he's gone.

"Ignore him," I say quickly. "He's forgetful. Mama says it's a miracle he memorized the Qur'an. He can never remember how old I am, much less what our band is called." I set my plate down. "You know what, I'm gonna go help with the stuff. I'll be right back." It's the only way to make sure my parents stay far, far away from the four of them as humanly possible until they go home. "I should also pray before time's up."

"Wait." Waleed uncrosses his legs and stands. "I'm coming, too. To pray, I mean. Not with you, obviously. But, like, your dad can lead, right?"

I'm so taken aback that all I can manage is, "Of course." The others follow us.

"Hey, Baba," I say, finding him rummaging around in the kitchen for plastic cups. "Have you read namaz yet? We were hoping you would lead."

Baba stops what he's doing and looks over at us in appreciation. "No, I haven't. I was just about to. Give me a few minutes."

We all use that time to take turns performing wudu in the hall bathroom. Baba leads the prayer with Waleed, Bilal, and Matthew behind him. Khadijah and I bring up the rear. When we finish, the five of us return to the basement to eat pizza and watch *The Greatest Showman*.

I reach for my sketchbook a few minutes in.

Khadijah peers down at my lap. "Are you bored?"

"No, I always do this. Helps me focus," I say, squinting because the TV screen's the only light I have right now.

Matthew looks over at me doubtfully. "Not paying attention helps you focus?"

"I *am* paying attention," I say without looking up.

"Nimra," Khadijah giggles. "Bilal just threw a paper cup at your head and you didn't even notice."

"Huh?"

Waleed laughs quietly to himself. "Qur'an, art, music. How do you fit everything inside your head? Tell us your secrets."

"Maybe she keeps them all in here." Bilal rips my sketchbook out of my hands. He spins it around in several directions, frowning. "What the heck is this?"

"I just started!" I protest. "I'm still setting up my grids."

Bilal wags his finger at me. "Let me show you how it's done." He helps himself to my pencil and starts marking up the page, screwing up his eyes in exaggerated concentration. With one last stroke, he flips it around for us to see.

"What is that?" I ask slowly.

"It's me," Bilal says like it's obvious. "It's one of those carrot chores."

This time, I laugh so hard I tear up. "You mean *caricatures*? It looks more like a balloon on a stick! You even forgot the ears."

"Let me." Khadijah steals the pencil and sketch pad from Bilal and draws elephant-sized ears on either side of his face. "There. That looks more like you."

"Not yet." Waleed takes it next and adds bushy eyebrows and buck teeth.

Matthew takes a turn and gives cartoon-Bilal spiky hair. "Now we're talking."

"You think you can do better?" Bilal seethes at them.

Khadijah scoffs. "Definitely. Nimra, do you mind?"

"Go ahead." They each borrow a pencil and blank page from the sketchbook. Everyone forgets the movie as they sit around and draw themselves.

"Wow. These are . . . terrible," I say when they proudly show me their sketches.

"How do we make them better?" says Matthew. "Teach us."

So I give them a crash course on the basics of sketching. We completely forget about the movie. They're so focused you'd think we were rehearsing for the band, except no one brings up Barakah Beats or the fundraiser. Mama and Baba don't check up on us again, so I finally relax. We talk, draw, laugh, and eat until it's time for them to leave.

It's the best evening of my life.

"Nice friends you have there, Nimmy," Baba says as he, Mama, and I wave goodbye at the door. "Good kids. You should invite them over more often."

I want to. I really do. When I'm with the guys and Khadijah, I feel like I can let go of everything and just be a normal kid.

But it could have been easily ruined if the Barakah Beats thing had come out. I can't be friends with them and keep hiding the band from Mama and Baba. I have to tell them the truth. It doesn't matter if they get mad at me. I can't have more fun days like today with the four of them if I'm always paranoid about my secret leaking. This is my chance. I can go right up to my parents and explain everything.

"Mama, Baba?" I say, trailing after them back inside the house. "There's this thing going on at ADAMS center Saturday after next. Can I go?"

"What kind of thing?" asks Mama.

My tongue ties. Will my parents still think my friends are good kids after I tell them about the music thing?

"It's a fundraising event," I say, my voice wobbling. "There's supposed to be this, um, talent show."

"A talent show?" Baba asks. "Are you going to recite the Qur'an?"

"No—" I start, but Mama interrupts.

"Of course she's not," she says. "She's just asking if she can *go*."

"Oh," Baba says. "Okay, sure. We were going to spend the entire weekend setting up at the warehouse and drop you off at Nano's, but we can drop you off at the fundraiser instead. Sorry that we can't join you, Nimmy."

Is this really happening? I can be in the talent show, fulfill my promise to the band, and my parents don't even have to find out! It's a win-win-win! I've never wanted to give them such a big hug in my whole entire life.

Baba claps me on the back. "I'm glad to see you're doing well, Nimmy. I know change is hard, but look how far you've come already. And it'll only get better from here."

Holy cow.

20

At school on Monday, I get cornered on my way to fifth block by two people—a boy in too-big glasses and a girl wearing a concert T-shirt I don't recognize.

"Hey, Nimra!" the girl says, walking beside me.

"Hi?" I say warily, worrying at my hijab from behind to make sure my hair isn't peeking out.

"Would you mind signing our agendas?" the girl asks, the words spilling out of her mouth so fast she practically trips over them. "We're huge fans of Barakah Beats."

"Waleed says you're the best thing to ever happen to the band. That you saved them from breaking up. He's friends with my friend's older brother. They have Tech Ed together," the boy says proudly.

Ugh, I've only been in a band for a few weeks and people are already making things up? What next? Dating rumors? Oh my gosh. NO. NO. My parents would literally kill me if they even smelled that one. I don't need this right now. Everything's finally going the way I want it to.

I stamp on the guilt my mind keeps throwing in my face. Just a little while longer, and it'll all be over.

Someone elbows me in the arm, and I flinch.

"Earth to Nimra," Jenna says, appearing out of the blue. She gestures to the boy and girl waiting in front of me. I stare at them, not remembering where I am or what they're doing here.

Jenna takes the agendas and pens they're holding out and pushes them into my hands. "Pull yourself together. Be cool," Jenna whispers. "You're gonna get this a lot from now on. Good to practice."

I blow out a sigh to calm the fear starting to grow in my chest. Then I uncap the pen and try to ignore the feeling that everything is about to blow up in my face.

*   *   *

People approach me from all sides throughout the day. I'm confused by the sudden fame, but by lunchtime I've gotten pretty good at making a run for it.

I find Khadijah in the cafeteria and ask her to sit with me and the other girls. She's always said no in the past, but the attention is starting to make me sick. I would feel better if she was there, too.

Unfortunately, Khadijah shakes her head. "No, thanks. I don't want to sit with them."

"Why not?" I ask impatiently. "They won't care."

"Yes, they will. I know them better than you, Nimra."

"That's not true!" I argue. "At least, I've known Jenna for a long time."

Khadijah puts her lunch box on the table in front of her. "Well, people change."

"What's your point?" I demand. Khadijah has no idea what she's talking about. Okay, yeah, I used Barakah Beats as an excuse to draw me and Jenna together again, but *still*. She just needed a reminder of how close we are. And it's working! I've known Jenna for years. Khadijah can't pass judgment on our relationship after only knowing me for a month.

Khadijah folds in on herself a little but doesn't back down. "It's up to you. Don't worry about me. I have company." She pats her lunch box, which has a book-shaped bulge in the front.

I open my mouth to respond, then turn on my heel and head to Jenna's table. I look back at Khadijah once before sitting down, and she seems sad. I don't get it! It's not like I'm leaving her to eat alone. She's choosing to do that on her own.

"Why isn't she coming?" Jenna asks, pointing her granola bar in Khadijah's direction.

"Doesn't feel like it," I say quietly.

"She never wants to talk to anybody," Val comments.

I want to come to Khadijah's defense, but Jenna gestures for me to sit. She's left a spot wide open next to her just for me.

"Did you sign any more autographs today?" Jenna asks curiously.

Her question bugs me. Why is the band the only thing she wants to talk about? I try changing the subject, but Val cuts in.

"Everyone's dying to hear the new song from you

guys," Val gushes. "The boys have been going around teasing about it."

Well, *that* explains why I've been getting bombarded from all sides today.

"You guys are still working on the one you're going to perform at that show, right?" Jenna asks. "Maybe I should come watch it, too. We can go together!"

My insides go cold. I'd normally be excited about Jenna wanting to come watch me, but bringing her to ADAMS with me is a no go. She'll spill the beans in the car, and then Mama and Baba will know everything.

"Did you help write the song?" Evelyn asks.

"I helped with lyrics," I say. "I don't play any instruments, so I did a lot of listening and word mixing."

The girls stare at me like I told them I won an Olympic gold medal. Something like dread spreads inside me. Jenna's welcomed me back into her circle again. They're all hanging on to my every word. Why am I not enjoying it?

"Are you really good friends with Waleed, Matthew, and Bilal now?" asks Julie. She takes a sip of apple juice.

"Yeah, we hung out at my house this weekend."

Jenna squeaks. "What? They were at your *house*? Why didn't you invite me over?"

"We had an away game," Evelyn reminds her. "You wouldn't have been able to go anyways. Coach would've killed you."

"Okay, but next time . . ." Jenna says, wagging a finger in my face. I blink. I want to go off that I *have* been inviting her over to my place for weeks! Suddenly, she wanted to be there because Barakah Beats was there, too? Where did all her other plans and excuses go?

"Who do you think is cuter?" Val asks.

I choke on my Ritz cracker. "Sorry?"

"Come on. You *must* like one of them. Who is it?" Val nudges my leg underneath the table. "Is it Waleed? Bilal? Don't say Matthew. He's Julie's."

"Shut up," Julie snaps, turning bright red.

"I'm just trying to help you! When are you going to quit being such a scaredy-cat?" Val turns to me.

"Leave her alone," says Evelyn. "How is Julie even supposed to talk to him?"

"I say we trip her into him in PE," Jenna says. "What do you say, Nimra?"

"No!" Julie panics.

"How else are you going to get his attention?" Jenna says.

"Morph into a guitar," I mumble. I'm not an expert on boys, but I have a feeling Matthew would just stare at Julie splat on the floor and keep walking. Bilal's more likely to help her up. "Matthew's kinda the more serious one."

Those simple words set Julie's hardened face alight.

"The serious guitarist. That's so hot," Val says, fanning her face.

I grimace. This conversation is *not* going the way I want it to.

Jenna puts her arm around me. "Help a sister out. Do you think you can talk to Matthew for Julie?"

Julie's anger turns to a look of hope, and suddenly it clicks into place: She only swallowed her pride and apologized because she'd get something out of it. Why didn't I realize it sooner?

But I'm one to talk. Maybe we can actually get along if I do this one nice thing for her. One less feud to feed the fifth circle of hell. Jenna'll like it if her other friends like me, too.

"I can try," I say.

I sneak a peek over my shoulder at Khadijah sitting alone. Her head is bent over her book, but I notice her eyes aren't moving across the page. She heard everything.

21

Mr. Peters blows the whistle like we're playing in the FIFA World Cup instead of a friendly game of seventh- versus eighth-grade soccer. Well, it's actually not so friendly. The older students have been making rude noises and egging us on since we started. We're being creamed.

It's almost October and the heat's finally letting up, but most of the boys and a handful of competitive girls in the seventh grade are still sweating buckets from their intense attempts to steal the ball. I hang around like a goalpost far away from all the action and panic every time the ball even comes near me. I manage to survive until we rotate players, and I'm finally allowed to take a break. Grass clings to my sweatpants as I sit down at the edge of the field that meets the track. Jenna and Julie come over, both sweat-slicked and grinning. *Athletes.* Only they could *enjoy* being sweaty.

"I almost scored that time," Jenna pants as she sits down. She spreads her pale legs out in front of her and rips out a handful of grass, then throws it in the air. "I was so *close.*"

"Yeah, but Matthew's good," Julie says breathlessly. She might have a crush on him, but she's not being biased. Bilal and Matthew are two of the best players. Matthew's the goalie and even though he's on the skinny side, no one can get the ball past him. And Bilal runs up and down the field with the ball like lightning.

"We were never actually going to beat them," I say. "The eighth graders would never let that happen." The whole middle school hierarchy would come toppling down if the seventh graders showed them up.

"I want to win, though," says Jenna. She has her game face on. I've watched enough of Jenna's home games to know when she's determined.

Meanwhile, all I can think about is getting out of here and having butter chicken for dinner.

A whistle goes off again, but this time it's Ms. O'Reilly's. "Okay, Cohen," she says to Matthew. "You're blocking so many that it's making this boring. Sit out. No, no trading places," she shouts when Matthew's teammates rise up in complaint. "You, too, Mohamed. Out. New goalie."

Matthew and Bilal trudge off the field, bummed to have been booted.

"Oh my gosh." Jenna puts on a wacky grin and nudges Julie. Winning the game has completely left her mind. "This is your chance, Jules! Go say hi!"

"No, he's with Bilal!" Julie squeals. "I can't just *go up to him*. What am I supposed to say?"

"Tell him you like their songs. Ask for an autograph."

Julie's dismay increases. "That's so extra."

"You're impossible," Jenna sighs, rolling her eyes. She looks past Julie at me expectantly. *Help her*, she mouths at me.

It's now or never. If I don't help Julie with this, Jenna will make me feel bad about it later. I just hope Matthew doesn't hate me for this.

"Follow me," I say. Jenna leaps up, dragging Julie with her. Julie's legs are shaking the whole way over to Matthew and Bilal. They're sitting shoulder to shoulder like two peas in a pod.

Bilal smiles when he looks up and sees me. "Hey, Nimz! That was a great play you made out there."

"What are you talking about? I didn't even touch the ball!"

"Yeah, I know," Bilal laughs. "You suck. It's a good thing you're a better singer."

Matthew lifts his head and winks through the pieces of hair falling into his eyes. "Sorry. We might be band-mates, but out here, we're rivals. Gotta put the seventh graders in their place. Assert our dominance."

"Funny. You guys weren't so tough when you butted heads dancing to Zac and Zendaya at my house." I clap my hands together for dramatic effect. They both laugh.

Jenna coughs behind me.

Oh. Right.

"Bilal, Matthew, these are my friends." My throat closes up around the word *friends*. Calling Julie that feels like a lie. I shake it off. "This is Jenna. And this is Julie." I pay special attention to Julie, whose ears are turning a scary shade of red. Jenna gives Julie an encouraging push from behind.

"H-h-hi," says Julie.

"Hey, you're the one who nearly hit me in the head," Matthew says, pointing at Jenna. "You play for real?"

Jenna beams at the unexpected attention. "No. I play volleyball. More hands than feet."

"Nice."

"Give me another chance and I'll score a goal on you. Mark my words," Jenna says confidently.

"You're on," says Matthew.

Julie rubs her bare arm with the opposite hand, looking defeated. A surprising surge of sympathy for Julie rises up inside me. I signal for her to say something. *Anything.* Julie's eyes slide between Matthew and Jenna, still talking smack about the game. Annoyed, I nudge Jenna's shin with my foot.

"Oh." She looks at Julie apologetically. "Well, I talk a big game, but Julie's got a mean pitching arm. She's captain of her softball team."

"That's cool," says Bilal.

He catches my eyes and gives me a questioning look. Discreetly, I flick my eyes at Julie, then Matthew. Bilal screws his face up, not understanding. I keep tennis-balling my gaze between them until it feels like my eyeballs are going to fall out.

When Bilal finally gets the hint, he shakes his head and mouths, *He's not interested.*

I groan, dragging my hands down my face.

Across the field, a cheer goes up from the seventh-grade side when they score a goal. Mr. Peters yells for players to rotate again.

"Cohen, Mohamed! You're up again," Ms. O'Reilly calls. "You, too, Birdie and Sharif!"

"Oh, it's on!" Jenna exclaims, running out. Seriously, who gets this excited about sweaty armpits? Matthew follows, his friends welcoming him back with open arms. Bilal looks over his shoulder at me, then at Julie apologetically.

I drag my feet to the edge of the field. I'm wondering if I'll lose points for not participating, when I see the ball flying in my direction. I scream, covering my head.

Out of nowhere, Julie jumps in front of me and sends it soaring across the field with a stupendous kick. It goes over everyone's heads—including Matthew's—and lands inside the net. Jenna stops, stunned. Our team cheers.

"Whoa. Thanks for saving my face," I say.

"Don't mention it." I expect her to run down the field to celebrate, but instead she sticks around to stand next to me.

"Sorry about—" I start.

Julie holds up her hand to cut me off. "No, it's okay. You tried. I'm the one who blew it. I still really appreciate that you tried to help, though. Honestly, I didn't think that you would do that for me. Not after how I treated you." Julie rubs the back of her flushed neck. "Look, I'm sorry about what I said in homeroom about you speaking English, and all the other mean stuff about your art. I shouldn't have judged you like that just because you're Muslim. Can we start over? For real this time?"

"If you keep the ball away from me forever, we're even." I stick out my hand. Julie smiles and we shake.

22

The next day is Evelyn's thirteenth birthday. Jenna, Julie, and Val are decorating her locker to surprise her.

Jenna tosses me a roll of pink streamers that I almost drop. Val and Julie smooth out shiny purple wrapping paper across the front of Evelyn's locker door. I feel like I should've brought Evelyn something, too, just to be nice, but Jenna only told me it was her birthday this morning.

"I made her favorite cupcakes," Val says. "Orange cream. Evelyn's the weirdo who likes orange-flavored stuff," she tells me. "My recipe is as good as it gets. I made enough for all of us." Val smiles in my direction. "You'll be there, right?"

"I don't know. We only have a few days left to practice before the show next week."

"You can blow off the band for a few minutes," says Jenna. "The guys won't mind. They're pretty chill." She says *the guys* like her short conversation with Matthew made them instant buddies. Julie catches me rolling my eyes and giggles. I hide my own grin. The air between us has been a lot lighter since PE yesterday. We even talked a little about art class this morning, which I hadn't known she was taking until she mentioned an exhibition coming up at the mall where middle schoolers' works would be displayed. It sounded so cool and I felt the familiar pang of frustration of having been left out.

The three of them finish decorating Evelyn's locker and clean up the scraps. I tug my backpack on when the bell rings for first block.

"Wait up, Nimra," says Jenna. She catches hold of my arm. "Can I come watch you practice in the band room today? Would that be weird?"

I narrow my eyes. "Are you sure it's *me* you want to watch?"

"Come on, you're my friend! *Please*. I just want to see what you guys do."

I'm super irritated. Maybe a month ago, I would have said yes. But now? I realize that I don't want to bring Jenna anywhere near Barakah Beats. They're two separate worlds that I don't want to cross over. It's wrong, like shading with the wrong pencil, or Spider-Man neglecting to help the little old lady cross the street.

"I don't think they'd like that," I lie. "They're pretty secretive."

Jenna's face falls. "Oh. Okay."

Out of the corner of my eye, I see Khadijah at her locker a few rows down. She meets my eyes, then quickly looks away. Our last conversation left things awkward between us for sure. I don't like it, but I don't know how to smooth things over. I never thought talking to Khadijah would be hard. She's, well, Khadijah.

A few minutes pass as I think about what to do. In the end, I give in to how hard my heart is tugging in Khadijah's direction and walk over to her.

"Hey," I say.

"Hey," she says in a voice softer than velvet. Khadijah looks down at the ground. "You should hurry. The tardy bell's about to ring."

"I know." I scratch the back of my hand. "I just— wanted to come say hi." *Smooth, Nimra.*

Khadijah offers a small smile. "I heard Jenna asking if she could come watch us practice. I don't think the guys would mind."

I don't respond. How do I explain to her that I don't want Jenna there without sounding like an awful friend?

Khadijah grabs her books out of her locker and closes the door. "You should know, they've done the same thing to me."

I blink. "Who did what to you?"

"Evelyn, Val, Julie, and Jenna," Khadijah says. "Last year they tried being nice to me and inviting me to their lunch table, but it was only because I'm Bilal's sister. You don't need those divas to be your friends. You have the guys. You have me."

Her words pierce my heart, which makes a lump rise in my throat. A part of me has always known that Jenna only came around because of the guys. I mean, that was my whole plan: join Barakah Beats so Jenna would see that I'm cool and start liking me again. But I also hoped Jenna wouldn't see it as the *only* reason to be my friend again. That she would remember all the good times we've had and want *me*. Nimra Sharif.

But then I remember what Julie said to me in PE: *I shouldn't have judged you like that just because you're Muslim.*

When Julie said that mean thing to me and then didn't want me to sit with them at lunch, Jenna let it happen. She should have stood up for me, but she never did. Ever since she thought I "forgot" to take my hijab off to go to school, Jenna's been making up all kinds of excuses for her rudeness. And unlike Julie, she hasn't once apologized to me for any of it.

It's almost like Jenna didn't care about hurting my feelings. Like she *agreed* with Julie's judgy comments. If my best friend can do all that without feeling bad, was she ever really my friend in the first place?

Maybe Khadijah is right. Maybe Nimra and Jenna's crime-fighting team is breaking up. The thought of letting go of Jenna *and* dropping out of the band after the talent show makes me feel like the ground's splitting beneath my feet. Even though I technically still "have" Jenna, it's not like it used to be. And now I'm wondering why I'm even trying to hold out for us when it feels like I'm the only who still cares about our friendship.

The Internet was right. Middle school sucks.

23

Nano and Nana invite us over for BBQ the Tuesday before the talent show with the rest of the family. I keep my distance from where my parents and grandparents are sitting, just in case they start arguing as usual. Instead, I hide out in the basement with my little cousins, who are playing on the Nintendo Switch.

Haris Mamou, Mama's youngest brother, let me borrow his tablet. I curl up on the couch to draw with a stylus while Arham, Huda, and Ayesha fight over who gets to play the next round.

"Nimra aapi!" Ayesha whines in her five-year-old voice. "They won't let me have a turn!"

"She's just going to lose after ten seconds anyway," Arham says. He's the oldest after me at nine years old, so he thinks he's the boss of everyone.

I remind him who's really in charge. "Arham, give Ayesha the controller," I command without lifting my eyes from the tablet.

But Arham won't be told what to do that easily. "Huda," he says to his other sister, "give Ayesha your controller."

The three of them start yelling over one another. I look helplessly over at Haris Mamou sitting on the opposite end of the couch with his laptop and headphones in, pointedly ignoring them.

Fine. I put my half-finished drawing of Spider-Gwen aside and initiate strict-mom mode. I hold out my hand and demand that Arham hand over the controller, then give it to his sister. Ayesha *does* manage to kill off her avatar in ten seconds, but at least it keeps her quiet until we all get called upstairs to eat.

Everyone gathered in Nano and Nana's kitchen appears normal. No signs of any problem. Just the usual here-and-there motions of setting out dishware and piling trays of food on the counter. My mouth salivates as I get in line behind my aunt while Baba and Nana transfer chicken and steak over from the grill. Nano makes my plate for me like I'm still little. I let her. I mean, Nano's basically like my second mom, and I like the exasperated look on Mama's face when she does it.

We sit down wherever there's a seat, with our plates in our laps just like we always do.

"So, Nimra," Mama's younger sister, Aanee, says. "Tell me all about your new school."

Dread suddenly starts to fray my stomach. "It's good," I say meekly. Except for the part where I'm still pretending like everything is normal with Jenna. I still eat lunch with her on B days and we walk to and from school together, but there's no spark. Honestly, being around her has become exhausting.

"Hah. No. I want details." Aanee pokes me in the side. "You know I went to Farmwell back in the day. You're probably going to have to do the mousetrap car in science, right? And the egg drop? They haven't changed those projects in forever."

"I guess?" I have no clue. My classmates talk about things that seem pretty obvious to them because it's just a fact they've known their whole lives. And I usually have no idea what's going on. Like this past Friday, Mr. Myer announced SAC elections and Khadijah had to whisper-explain to me what SAC even was from across the aisle.

"Have you thought about joining any clubs?"

"Haan, good idea," says Nano. "Like Science Olympiad. Or robotics. I've heard a lot about both of them. You should look into sports as well. It's no good being locked up inside all the time. Dedicate your time to learning things that will be useful."

I look down at my plate. Is my love of drawing *useless* just because it won't make me a doctor or athlete? I've been getting better at sharing my pictures. People are actually looking at them. It's not *useless*.

"She's only twelve. And it hasn't even been that long," Mama says to Nano. "Let her settle down a bit more."

"You mean she's *already* twelve, and it's taken this long for you to let her see the face of a real school. Bechari, you and Saim have kept her from having a normal life like all the other kids. If you care about your daughter's future at all, you'll stop going easy on her."

"Or what?" Mama snaps, dropping her fork. "She'll end up like me?"

My hand freezes in place, my glass of water halfway to my mouth. I look at Mama, whose eyes are glassy with fury. *Here we go.*

"Stop projecting your grievances against me onto her," Mama says. "I get it, okay? You're disappointed that I left my job to raise Nimra and never went back. You still can't face the fact that your American-raised, college-educated daughter chose to be a stay-at-home mom rather than work myself to death trying to do everything like you did."

I wish I could turn invisible. *Why is it always about me?*

Nano purses her lips. She looks a lot like Mama when she's irritated. "Your sister hasn't missed a day of work since she had kids," Nano says, raising her spoon in accusation. "I haven't been without a job since you were in elementary school and you all turned out just fine. Everybody does it. Everybody *can* do it. I warned you not to leave such a huge gap in your résumé. You could have gone so far in your career."

"And what I am now is nothing?" Mama yells. "A

good mother who's always been there when her kid needs her? Someone who doesn't just throw materialistic junk in her face to make up for my lack of actual parenting? I've always given her the kind of moral support you never gave me. All you wanted to do was control my life."

"All right, that's enough—" Baba says, but no one is listening to him.

Nano gives Mama a painted-on smile. "You think you're being a good parent. What you're really doing is making up excuses for your laziness and unwillingness to work hard and setting a bad example for Nimra. What you and Saim are doing with the business is not guaranteed to last. I don't want Nimra to be like you."

Mama is on her feet now, staring down at Nano with her fists quivering at her sides. "And I don't want her to be like *you*. All you care about is worrying about what other people think of you instead of how your own children feel. You never once stopped to consider how it impacted us. But I'm not you. Since the day I found out about Nimra, I refused to be like you."

"Ya Allah, Maryam, you are so—"

"Everybody SHUT UP!" I yell.

My voice doesn't have the power I was going for, but it still cuts through the house, shocking my cousins and the adults. Staying quiet through these fights and pretending like I can't hear them has always been my way of coping. But this was the last straw.

"Why do you always pretend like I'm not *sitting right here*? I can think for myself!"

Mama and Nano stare at me in shock. Aanee reaches for my hand, but I slam my plate of mostly untouched food down on the coffee table and bolt upstairs. I lock myself in Aanee's old room and hide underneath the covers. I smush my runny nose into the pillow and lie like that for what seems like forever. I don't respond to all the knocks begging me to open the door or the voices asking if I'm okay: Mama, Baba, Nano, Aanee, and even Haris Mamou. I just cry and sleep, cry and sleep, until the sun goes down.

When I finally lift my head over the covers, it's dark inside. Face covered in snot, I sit up on the edge of the bed. My stomach growls, but I ignore it. Downstairs is mostly quiet, and I wonder where everyone is and what they must be doing. I've never shouted like that before, much less at adults.

I pick up my phone, fingers trembling. I have a few unread messages on WhatsApp from when I was angry-sleeping.

> **Waleed:** Ok, gang. I recorded our last session and worked all day to put this together. What do you think of this demo?

Below it is an attached sound file. The others have already listened to it.

> **Matthew:** Not bad!
> **Bilal:** COOL
> **Khadijah:** I LOVE IT!!!
> **Waleed:** Nimra?

Waleed sent that last text over an hour ago. I press play on the clip.

The instrumental that fills the darkened bedroom is beautiful. No, it's *powerful*. It's exactly the mood we were going for. Waleed nailed it. I listen to it again, mouthing the lyrics from memory, my and Bilal's voices filling the empty spaces.

Despite everything, the music makes me feel . . . better. I helped create this. It might not be my usual creative outlet, but it still brings me that sense of achievement that sketching does. When you look at your hard work and are proud of pulling it off.

You're not supposed to be proud of it. It's wrong.

> **Bilal:** Nimz probably went to bed. I can't wait for everyone to hear this! Waleed, you should upload it to SoundCloud.
>
> **Waleed:** On it.

Fear sparks in my belly. The whole school's going to hear the song, hear me sing. They'll share it with their friends, who will share it with everyone they know, and next thing it will reach Mama and Baba. I can already imagine the upset look on their faces when the truth comes out. The fight downstairs replays in my mind on loop. There's this permanent wedge superglued between

Mama and Nano because Nano can't bring herself to accept that Mama chose a different life from the one she wanted for her. And I might doom myself to the same fate by being a part of something *I don't even feel good about.* What's *wrong* with me?

I'm done. I can't go through with the talent show. I can't let Barakah Beats split up me and my parents. I won't. I have to tell the boys I'm dropping out. Tomorrow. It'll shatter them, but there's no other way. At the end of the day, I'm going to have to let someone down.

I fall backward on the bed and half groan, half scream into my hands.

No matter what I do, I'm always disappointing someone. But as bad as it feels to let Mama and Baba or the guys down, it feels even worse to disappoint myself.

24

As I expected, Waleed is *not* happy when I tell him I'm not going to practice as we walk out of algebra the next day.

"What the heck?" he wails. Waleed stares like he's waiting for me to reveal it's one big prank. "This is the absolute wrong day. Wrong week! Nimra, we can't rehearse without you. Your part's so important."

My cheeks flush pink. "Sorry, I just don't feel good." Really, I'm buying myself some time to figure out how I'm going to tell the guys that I'm dropping out of the talent show. I haven't been able to focus in any of my classes all day. The stress is eating me alive. Something's telling me it's gonna get ugly. But the band will have to learn to survive without me.

Waleed puts his head between his hands, messing up his hair in the process. "We only have two days left to practice! I *knew* we should've practiced that weekend instead of goofing off at your house."

"Hey! It was fun. I don't regret it. We needed the break."

"Break from what? We haven't done enough!" Waleed groans. "Why aren't you taking this seriously?"

I narrow my eyes at him. It was one thing for him to complain about me missing rehearsal, but I won't let him accuse me of not doing my part. "You know what, Waleed? I get that this show is important to you, but you need to stop yelling at me. It's unprofessional and . . . and . . . mean!"

With that, I spin on my heel and head straight for the cafeteria.

Jenna waves a baby carrot in the air when she sees me. "Hey, what are you doing here? Aren't A days band days?"

"Yeah, I'm, uh, really hungry and wanted to eat first," I say. My hands shake as I take out my chicken roll.

"You guys' new song is amazing," Julie says excitedly.

Waleed shared the demo on SoundCloud last night, but I didn't bother to check it out. Mostly because I didn't do anything when we got home from the disastrous BBQ except drive myself bonkers over how I was going to come clean to Khadijah and the guys in a way that wouldn't end badly. Meanwhile, Mama and Baba pretended like nothing had happened. It was like awkwardly patting someone on the back after punching them in the face.

"Everyone's been talking about it," Evelyn says. "I listened to it on repeat for hours while I was doing my homework. You have such a pretty voice!"

"Thanks, I, uh—" I sputter. My eyes flick to the clock. *Slow down, time!* The girls eat and continue dissecting the new song while my chest squeezes tighter and tighter as the clock tick-tocks toward my doom. Finally, I can't stall any longer. I take a deep, shaky breath. I'll never be ready. It's now or never.

I pack up my lunch, say goodbye to Jenna and the others, and head for the band room. Every step feels like my ankles are chained to a boulder. I want to turn around and run right out of the building. *You can do this,*

Nimra, I think as my eyebrows start to sweat. *Just get it over with.*

I stop short when I hear shouting coming from the main band room.

"YOU'RE OFF-KEY!"

"I AM NOT! YOU'RE NUTS!"

"BOTH OF YOU KNOCK IT OFF!"

I hesitate before throwing the doors open and freeze at the scene in front of me. Waleed and Bilal are standing toe-to-toe glaring at each other. Between them, Matthew is holding his precious guitar over his head like he can't decide whose head to bash in first. Khadijah's staring at everyone helplessly.

"Look who decided to show up," Waleed snaps.

"What's going on?" I say.

"Just Waleed being his usual controlling self," says Bilal. "What else is new?" I've never seen him look so upset. Usually, Waleed's outbursts roll right off him.

"He's being a pain," Matthew agrees. "He's criticizing everything. How many times do we have to do the same thing over and over? We're ready!"

"No, we're not!" says Waleed.

"THEN WE NEVER WILL BE!" Bilal drops into a chair with his back to his friend. Matthew claws at his face with one hand like he's biting back a scream. Barakah Beats is falling apart right before my eyes.

"Listen," I say carefully. I'm afraid one wrong word is going to set someone off again. "You guys are fighting for no reason."

"Yeah, tell that to him." Bilal jerks his head at Waleed.

"The song is good. Our singing is great. What more do you want?" I ask Waleed. "We're not professionals. We're doing a fundraiser show. The point is to help out and have fun while doing it. That's it."

"You didn't even show up for rehearsal," Waleed says sharply. "Don't pretend you care."

I know it's just his stress talking, but his words hurt anyway. "I *do* care. We all do," I say, gesturing to the rest of the band. "Not just you."

"We created this band because we love music and want to share it with other people," Matthew says. "It's never been about winning a competition."

"That's because I'm the only one who wants bigger things for us!"

I throw my hands up. "For goodness' sake, Waleed, you're still in middle school. Relax!"

He shakes his head. "I thought you would understand, Nimra. That you'd take my side. But you're just like the rest of them. You're not committed—"

And just like that, I've had enough. I risked everything to be a part of this band, and Waleed's just gonna go and single me out like that? Everything in my life is out of control. The lies, the talent show, my family, Jenna—they all crash together in my head . . . and explode out of my mouth.

"You know what, Waleed? You're right. I don't care about your stupid music or this band. It's stupid and wrong! Do you even know that Islam forbids making music? This is not okay! None of this is okay!"

From far away, I hear what I just said . . . and cringe. But even though my mind is telling me to stop, my mouth doesn't get the memo—I'm on a roll now and there's no holding me back.

"And you know what else?" I hear myself say. "I only agreed to join you guys and do the show because it made me look cool in front of my friend!"

I cover my mouth in horror as soon as the words are out, but it's too late. Silence chokes the room. Bilal and Khadijah stare at me, mouths gaping. Matthew's white as a sheet. Waleed's expression contorts in a way that breaks my heart.

"What do you mean?" Bilal asks softly.

My heart squeezes in my chest. I knew I had to tell them the truth, but I can't believe it's happening like *this*. Why couldn't I have kept my mouth shut?

"I've been lying to you. To everyone. My parents, too. They don't know about Barakah Beats, or that it's the reason I hang out with you guys. I hid it from them, just like I hid the real reason I agreed to join the band."

I can feel their disappointment burning a hole in the side of my face. The urge to break down is so strong, but I don't deserve to cry. I hurt *them*, not the other way around.

"I'm sorry," I say, my voice wobbling. "I'm sorry I used you, and I'm sorry I let it get this far. I never should have agreed to do the show." I take a shaky breath. "I'm dropping out."

Waleed throws his hands up in the air. "Wait, so that's it? You're gonna go all Zayn from One Direction on us and bail? After that little speech about how I should think about the rest of the group?"

"I have to," I say, walking backward toward the door, eyes glued to the floor. "I'm sorry to be such a crappy bandmate."

"You aren't just a crappy bandmate," Khadijah says. "You're a crappy friend."

I turn on my heel and run out of the band room. No one comes after me.

*   *   *

Everyone's throwing their trash away when I reenter the cafeteria, trembling from head to toe. I stare into space with unfocused eyes. My ears sound like they're full of cotton. I fight to keep it together or I'll end up on the ground hugging my knees to my chest, where my heart is trouncing like a wild animal desperate to escape.

Kids jostle me as I walk in the opposite direction of the crowd, scanning the room for a familiar platinum-blonde head. For the only person in the whole school who, despite everything, I know when it comes down to it, I can count on. Jenna catches sight of me first and comes over, swinging her empty lunch box. "Hey, Nimra. Whoa, what happened? Why do you look like that?"

"I—" I'm about to say I'm fine, but even thinking it makes me wince. No more lies. I gulp. "I broke up with the band. I'm not in Barakah Beats anymore."

"*What?*" Jenna screeches, her eyes widening. "Why?"

Before I can answer, Principal Coggins notices we're still there and starts making shooing gestures at us. "Ladies, please, no dawdling. Off you go."

Jenna grabs my arm and leads me out the side doors to the dark and narrow lunch detention hallway next to the cafeteria. With a single long table, it's basically the entrance to the back storeroom and garbage disposal. When we're alone, Jenna rounds on me. "Okay, tell me what happened."

"We got into a fight," I explain, sinking onto the bench. "It was my fault. I wasn't being totally honest with them about something, and I thought I could keep it a secret, but it bit me in the butt instead. Now they hate me and will probably never speak to me again. It's over."

"Nimra, you're overreacting. Bandmates fight all the time! What was the fight about? The song?"

"No, I—I didn't feel like I was being true to myself by being in the band," I say. "I feel like I had to leave."

"Were they jerks about it? Come on, you gotta give me more here! What was their reaction? I'm sure if you apologize, they'd let you back in." Jenna sounds like a paparazzo who follows celebrities around looking for the scoop, not like someone trying to comfort a friend. And maybe that's what I've been to her this whole time. A connection to people who are, in her eyes, worth more than me.

"Why do you care more about them than the fact that I'm upset?" I say.

Jenna's facial muscles knot themselves in confusion. "I'm trying to help you, but I can't do that if I don't know the whole story."

My face blazes. Here I am saddled with guilt and all she wants are the exclusive details. I thought coming to her would restore some of my confidence, that she would still like me for me even after losing these cool eighth-grade boys as my friends. She let me down.

I can't believe I joined the band and lied to my parents for her. All I'd hoped for was a hug or an *It's okay, I'm here for you.* Apparently, I was asking for too much.

"You know what, Jenna?" I say, looking her straight in the eye. "I'm not telling you anything more about the band. Because I'd only share that with a *real* friend, and you're not that. You barely paid any attention to me for weeks, not since you realized I was going to wear my hijab to school. It was easy for you to hide what you really thought about me being Muslim when it was just us two, but that changed when you had to start hanging out with me in public." My voice shakes a little, but I keep going. I need to say this to her. "I'm not going to be friends with someone who doesn't care about me for who I am. You might be embarrassed by it, but *I'm not*. Now if you'll excuse me, I have to go to Spanish."

With that off my chest, I march out of there, my heart shattering into a million pieces over losing everyone I care about in one lunch period.

25

"Nimra, you can't stay in there forever," Mama says from the other side of my closed bedroom door.

"Watch me," I say from the bed.

Yesterday after I stormed home from school, I stuffed my bag full of water and Oreos, collected all my art supplies from the basement, and locked myself in my room . . . which is where I'm going to live out the rest of my life. At least until I run out of Oreos, anyway. At the rate I've been scarfing them down, I've got a day at most before I have to crawl out of my hole to restock. Mama sighs. "You'll have to come out at some point."

Nervousness briefly breaks through my misery, but I push it back down. "I don't want to."

"Don't you think you're being a little dramatic?" Mama says.

"I'm twelve! I'm allowed to be dramatic. Now leave me alone."

"I was never this theatric at her age," Mama whispers to someone—it can only be Baba. He gave up trying to get through to me after I refused to wake up for school this morning. I check my phone—it's just about time for everyone to be heading into sixth block. Jenna hasn't texted once since I lashed out at her. My WhatsApp chat with the band is crickets, too. "I'm sure your parents remember differently," Baba responds on the other side of the door. "Tweens, you know. Everything is tragic."

I pull the covers over my head to cancel out their concerned voices. "Go away!"

"Give her time," Baba says gently. "Let us know when you're ready to talk, Nimmy." I imagine him putting his hand on Mama's shoulder and tugging her away from the door.

I sit up when their footsteps recede downstairs. Crumbs litter my bed and I brush them off. My hair is a disaster. Still in my pajamas, I sit down at my desk and flip to a blank page in my sketchbook. I blow a strand of hair out of my face, glaring down at the empty canvas. Jenna's annoying face fills my vision as I attack it with lead. And past Nimra's face, too. Past Nimra's even worse. She's the reason I'm here in the first place. I hate her, that liar.

I let my hand do whatever it wants. When I finally look up, my eyes hurt from concentrating too hard. I jump at the five drawings staring back at me. A book, a microphone, a guitar, a keyboard, and a pencil.

Khadijah, Bilal, Matthew, Waleed, and me. Longing pangs my stomach. I'm starting to have a headache, too. I've missed every single prayer since Zuhr yesterday. I rub at my face, fingers leaving smudges.

My chair creaks loudly as I back out of it and go to the bathroom to make wudu. But instead of praying, like I should be doing, I retrieve my copy of the Qur'an from my bookshelf—the pink one Mama gave me—and make my bed to sit cross-legged with a pillow in my lap and a scarf around my head.

Sister Sadia once told me, *If you're down, just read. Whenever you need its comfort most, it will speak to you.* I'm not in the mood to do that, but I'm pretty down right now and not even drawing is helping . . . so I might as well try.

I open the Qur'an at the very beginning, close my eyes, and start reciting from memory.

My voice is hoarse, unused to the Arabic after so many weeks. I have to cheat by looking ahead several times. I've become so bad at even the one thing I used to be so good at, a talent that made me stand out and made my family proud. Tears spring to my eyes; my voice cracks. I hang my head between my shoulders, the misery eating me up inside as I cry. I miss never questioning where I belonged. I miss not having to do wrong things to make other people happy. I wish I hadn't lied to anyone or changed into someone I can't stand to get Jenna back.

A hand squeezes my shoulder. I look up in surprise to find Mama and Baba standing over me. I must've forgotten to lock my door.

Baba says, "Nimmy, what's wrong?"

That only makes me cry harder. "I want my old life back!"

"Did something happen at school?" Mama asks, dropping down beside me on the bed. She covers my hands with hers, and it's like a key unlocking everything I've kept bottled up inside. It all comes rushing out: the first day of school, Jenna shunning me, Barakah Beats, Khadijah, and every lie that got easier to tell.

Mama and Baba are still as statues when I finish. "Why on earth didn't you come to us before?" Mama asks. She sounds so let down.

"I never thought it would go this far! I thought I could stop whenever I wanted to, but it was like being under a magic spell. I didn't feel or act like myself. It was awful."

"That is still no excuse for what you did," says Baba. "You should never have lied to us, or your friends."

I bury my face in my hands. "God hates me, doesn't he?"

"No." Mama lifts my head and forces me to look at her. "Allah doesn't hate you. But you know what? He would be disappointed if you went back on your word."

It takes a second for her meaning to hit. "You're saying I should do the show with Barakah Beats? You don't think it's wrong?"

"You should never have made a promise you didn't intend on keeping," Baba says. "You owe those boys and Khadijah an apology, and I don't see a better way to make it up to them. As long as you learned your lesson. Honestly, it sounds to me like you were using the whole music thing as an excuse to cover up the bigger problem here, Nimmy. If you were having friend problems, you could've told us. We would've helped you. You know that."

"I know," I say, ashamed.

"Then why didn't you?"

"Because you guys were happy thinking everything was great. I didn't want you to know that it was all fake. And I was scared if you found out that . . . that you would be so disappointed in me and we would fight how you and Nano always do. I didn't want us to turn out like that. I thought you would hold the music thing against me because it's not something we do."

Mama's shoulders droop, pressed down by a familiar weight. "Oh, Nimra. I'm so sorry you felt that way." She wraps her arms around me. "Listen to me. Don't ever think you can't share things with us. One of the biggest reasons why parents and their children end up in a bad place is because they don't communicate or work through their disagreements together."

"I guess you and Nano never really did that, huh?" I say.

"No, honey. The enemy of compromise is stubbornness. Your grandparents are disappointed that I didn't choose to live my life the way *they* wanted me to live it, but then I wouldn't have been able to spend as much time with you. I chose to stay home because it's what I decided was right for *me*. You and I can have our differences, and that's *okay*. It doesn't mean I'll stop loving you."

"Everyone has to figure out their own path," Baba says. "I'm proud of your mama for finding hers, especially when times were tough."

"You were too little to realize it at the time," says Mama, "but I went through postpartum depression after you were born. That's when new mothers get very sad after the birth of their baby. And my parents' expectations only made it worse."

"How did you get better?" I ask softly.

"Well, we couldn't afford counseling. But you know what did help me cope?" Mama smiles. "Music. I know Islam has many different interpretations about music, and I think they're all equally valid. What's most important is that you understand what your intentions are. If you're worried it's going to lead you to do the wrong thing, then don't do it. I hope Allah can forgive me if He found anything wrong in the choices that I made."

Mama's words make me feel bad all over again. "My intentions weren't good. I messed up."

"What do you think you should do to fix it?" Baba says. "What do you *want* to do? Be honest. We're on your side, Nimmy. Never forget that."

The ball's in my court now. No strings attached. For the first time in a while, I look deep inside, searching for the answer. I joined the band to please Jenna. I stayed in the band to please the guys. I dropped out of the talent show to please my parents. But where had I, Nimra, been in this whole fiasco? It's time I figure out what *I* need to do, and there's only one option. There has always been only one choice that my heart will accept.

"I don't want to be in the band," I say. "But I don't want to lose my friendship with the boys and Khadijah."

"Then you know what you need to do," Baba says.

He's right—I *do* know what I need to do. But the thought of confronting Waleed, Matthew, Bilal, and Khadijah terrifies me. Especially when I imagine what they probably think of me now. I wish I could go back in time and undo everything. Start over, do the right thing, do what Baba told me on the first day of school. *Just be yourself.* This whole time, I was convinced Jenna was the *right* friend when I really should have focused on who was my *true* friend.

I just hope Khadijah and the guys can forgive me.

"Mama, Baba," I say, looking at them with as much gratitude as I can muster. "Thank you for understanding."

"Now, wait a minute," says Mama. "You did lie to us and that does warrant a punishment."

I groan. Should've known I wasn't getting off that easy.

"You have to help sort orders downstairs and take them to the post office with us."

I groan again.

"It's not *all* bad," Baba says. "Tell her the rest."

Mama grins. "We're so proud of how dedicated you are to your art, and that's why we decided we're also okay with you taking art in school next year. But it had better not distract you from other subjects."

I almost fall off the bed. "SERIOUSLY?" Happy tears spring to my eyes. I tackle my parents in the biggest hug I've ever given anyone. "Oh my God, thank you! I promise

I'll stay focused in my other classes. It won't change anything. This is the best!"

"Come on, Nimmy. The work's not gonna do itself."
Baba lifts me up and carries me out of the room with my
arms wrapped around his neck while I scream excitedly.
Mama yells at both of us to be careful going down the
stairs.

26

My parents are nice enough to write me a note for coming into school late on Friday, even though I skipped all of yesterday. I wanted to talk to my friends right away, so I couldn't possibly pay attention to my morning classes when my whole mind would've been on what I'm going to say to the band.

Mama and Baba drop me off five minutes before lunch. I check in at the main office and head straight for the band room, my breath shaking the whole way.

I'm shocked to discover the room is empty. They should be in here by now. Feeling queasy, I cross over to the cafeteria and peer inside. Waleed, Matthew, and Bilal are at the same table as the first time I saw them, surrounded by their eighth-grade friends. Khadijah is reading at the end of a different table all by herself.

What are they doing in here? They should be rehearsing.

For a brief moment, my gaze lands on the back of Jenna's head and my heart shrinks with regret. But right then, I realize Waleed, Matthew, and Bilal are staring at me. Their expressions range from hurt to angry to confused. Khadijah raises her head and pins me with her eyes, too. My embarrassment is brutal. I feel tethered by their gazes. They all look away at once, cutting me loose, and I float away . . . right back down to earth.

I cast Jenna out of my head as I step out into the hallway and whip my phone out. I open the Barakah Beats WhatsApp chat and type, EMERGENCY MEETING IN THE BAND ROOM. After a few seconds I add, Please? and send it to the group.

I wait in the band room, more and more discouraged with every minute that passes without anyone showing up. Maybe what I did was unforgivable. Maybe they never want to talk to me again. If that's what they decide, I'll have to accept it. But I really, really hope they don't.

Just when I'm about to give up, the door opens. I stand, hope coursing through my veins when the four of them walk in together. They look uneasy, not sure if they should have come. Nobody says anything for the longest time. We're all breathing awkward instead of oxygen. Then Bilal finally breaks the silence.

"So . . . what's the emergency?" he asks.

"It's our last A day before the show," I say. "We should be practicing!"

They exchange looks with one another.

"We're not playing at the fundraiser anymore," Matthew says. "We pulled out."

My stomach dips. "Why?"

"Because the song was written for two singers. Matthew has to focus on guitar, and even with the background riffs, Waleed still has to play keyboard. We tried to see what it would sound like if he took over your part, but it wasn't the same."

"It was *ruined*," Waleed says wretchedly. "I can't match your voice. I'd rather not play than embarrass ourselves in front of everyone. So we dropped out. It's over."

This feels like a punch to the gut. I promised myself

I wouldn't cry in front of them, but I can't help it. I'm the reason why all our hard work will go to waste. It shouldn't be like this.

"I'm sorry," I say, tears in my eyes. "For everything. For lying. I shouldn't have said that stuff to you guys about playing music being wrong. But I was mad and stressed and—"

Waleed holds up his hand to stop my apology. "We just want to know one thing. Was it always about your friend? Did you have to force yourself to hang out with us every single time? Did you even like us?"

"Of course I like you guys! I never had to force myself. Ever. Jenna might've been the reason why I joined Barakah Beats, but you guys are the reason why I stayed. You're talented and funny and nice, and you made me feel like a part of the group. I wanted to tell you the truth so many times. I'm sorry I didn't. I'm really, really sorry."

Matthew speaks up. "What you said about Islam forbidding music. I asked my parents about it. They said people have different opinions, and that I wasn't doing anything wrong. I can keep making music."

I nod. "I had no right to say that to any of you. I

shouldn't have judged you. If you want to play music, then you should. But . . . I meant what I said about it not being right for me. I don't want to pretend to be someone I'm not anymore." I take a deep breath and remember what Mama said about Allah, and how He feels about breaking promises. "The thing is, I don't want to be the reason we don't perform. So just this once . . . I want to sing with you for the fundraiser. Is it too late?"

"Your parents are okay with it?" Matthew asks.

"Yes. It's for a good cause."

Waleed rubs his forehead. "We might be able to get back in the program if we move fast," he says. "If everyone's on board for *real* this time."

"I am," I say confidently. "Completely on board."

"If you're in, so am I," Khadijah pipes up. She gives me a kind smile I don't deserve. "It's okay. We all make mistakes."

"Me, too," Bilal says, putting his hand on her shoulder. "Team Barakah Beats."

"Team Barakah Beats," echoes Matthew.

Waleed finally breaks. A kindle of something—hope—lights up in his eyes. "Team Barakah Beats!"

"Now that we're back on . . . I have something for you. I kept it in case you changed your mind." Khadijah digs through her bag and hands me a T-shirt. It's the band T-shirt she ordered with my artwork on it for the talent show.

I hug it to my chest. "Thank you," I say, my eyes filling with tears. "I just want you to know that I'm not interested in being your friend because you're Bilal's little sister. I like you because you're Khadijah and you were there for me when no one else was."

Khadijah throws her arms around me. I sink into the hug, and for the first time in more than a month, I don't miss Jenna.

"Nimz, I hate to break it to you, but we know you're lying. It's *definitely* because she's my little sister," Bilal teases. Khadijah elbows him in the ribs, and I laugh.

"So . . . friends?" I ask.

Waleed grins. "Friends."

"Then what are we waiting for?" Matthew says excitedly. "We've got a show to win! Let's get practicing."

"Don't mean to kill the mood, but there are literally five minutes left of lunch," Khadijah says.

"After school, then. At my house," Waleed offers.

"And Nimra shouldn't have to do anything she's uncomfortable with. I still want her to sing, but we can make a few adjustments to the song. I have an idea."

"No, no, I owe you," I argue. "It's okay. Don't worry about me."

Waleed shakes his head. "Trust me. I think you guys will like what I've got up my sleeve." Waleed nudges Matthew. "That is, if you're up for another part."

Matthew looks at him suspiciously. "What exactly do you have in mind?"

27

"Barakah Beats?" The ADAMS volunteer addresses us from over his clipboard. "You're on after this act. You ready?"

"Yes," we say in unison. He ticks something off on his sheet and whispers into his earpiece as he strides off.

When he's gone, Bilal says, "I can't believe they put us last." He picks at his shirt collar anxiously. "I'm sweating. Is anyone else sweating? I need water."

I pass Bilal a bottle from the cooler kept backstage for the contestants. He gulps it down quickly, splashing water on the front of his shirt. We're all wearing the matching T-shirts, including Khadijah. She says she wants to show her support once she joins the audience.

Which is huge. One peek around the curtains shows us that the community came out in full force tonight for the fundraiser. Even hidden in shadows, I can see Mama and Baba got good seats in the middle of the auditorium. They put their work stuff on hold so they could come. Nano and Nana are here, too, and Aanee, and my uncles and little cousins. Sister Sadia and lots of other familiar and new faces sit in the crowd, too, watching the current act. It's a brother/sister slam poetry pair and they're incredible. There have been magic tricks, and short films, and comedians, and so many other talents that each one made us more nervous than the last.

"I should go sit down. Good luck, guys." Khadijah gives us a thumbs-up. "You're going to blow them away." She takes off after one last encouraging smile.

Matthew hugs his guitar close. "This is it. The moment we've all been waiting for."

"I'm gonna faint," says Bilal.

"Don't you dare!" Waleed laughs, but I can tell he's nervous, too. At this point, we know the song and our routine like the backs of our hands. But it's one thing to practice among ourselves and a whole other thing to perform in front of our friends, family, and strangers. Lots of strangers. And religious leaders. Oof.

I hop on one foot, then the other. I'm thirsty, but I don't want to have to pee in the middle of our performance.

The siblings onstage wrap up and the audience cheers for them while they bow.

"Wow! That was amazing!" The bearded emcee walks onstage from the other side. "Let's give them one more round of applause!" More cheering and clapping. "Okay, folks. We're almost at the end of our program. We've seen so many incredible talents tonight. It speaks to the awesomeness of our beautiful, diverse community. On behalf of ADAMS and from the bottom of my heart, I thank you for your support. Please know that your donations will make a huge impact on resettling refugee families. Hold tight, now. I know everyone's hungry. Dinner will be served momentarily. We've got one last act."

"Great. They're all gonna be daydreaming about food instead of paying attention to us," whispers Matthew.

"From Farmwell Station Middle School," the bearded emcee says onstage, "please put your hands together for Barakah Beats!"

"Let's give it everything we have," I say. "No matter what happens, we do our best." We fist-bump as a group and the emcee waves us on.

Bilal and I are handed microphones, while Waleed sets up his keyboard. We take formation: Matthew perched on a stool with his guitar in the back left, Waleed standing behind his keyboard to the right, me and Bilal center stage. The stage lights are hot. My hand shakes as I look out into the audience, sweat tickling my upper lip.

The audience is quiet, waiting. I close my eyes, feeling my bandmates' presence around me. I open them again, and I see Khadijah beaming up at us. Mama and Baba lean forward in their seats. They nod reassuringly.

Bilal gives the people backstage the cue and we're officially on. Speakers on either side of the stage spill our instrumental mix. Matthew meets the melody with his guitar and Waleed introduces the keyboard exactly where we planned. I listen intently, counting down in my head until Bilal's part.

He starts singing, and I'm completely engulfed by the music and the narrative we created between two kids— the boy praying for the safety of his brothers and sisters fleeing their homes overseas, and the refugee girl cross-ing paths with him as she arrives in a new land, having sacrificed everything to start over. Bilal and I are in per-fect sync the whole time. We're better than we've been in rehearsal. The music flows through the air effortlessly, our voices intermingling with it like wind in the per-fect storm. The audience feels its effect, too. They listen, enraptured.

We reach the end of the song and the music dies, but no one moves. Something in the air must indicate to the crowd that we aren't finished.

They're right.

Waleed, Matthew, and Bilal melt into the background, and I'm left standing center stage, facing the jam-packed room in silence. The lights dim, spotlighting me. When Waleed first told me his idea, I was speechless. The others loved it so much that it didn't take much begging on their part to get me to agree. Waleed's dad helped me prepare for exactly this moment while I was at their house yesterday.

The boys start humming in the background a cappella. A swell of power rises up in my throat and, with all eyes on me, I begin to recite Surah Yasin, the heart of the entire

Qur'an. After discussing it, we decided this was the chapter that fit the overall story we were trying to tell. The chapter Muslims read in memory of those we've lost.

I don't just read it. I sing it with everything inside me. I hit all the right beats. My voice reaches new heights, echoing around the room with a fierce clarity I didn't know I could achieve. Nobody expected this. Several people in the audience cover their mouths in amazement. Dozens of eyes begin to water. Mama and Baba, holding each other's hands, beam proudly.

The guys' vocals trail off with me as I finish. I lower the microphone, out of breath, staring out at a sea of bewildered faces. Then, thunderous applause. Louder than any other act got tonight. The crowd jumps to its feet in a standing ovation.

Waleed, Bilal, and Matthew step into line beside me and, together, we bow.

"You gave me goose bumps," Khadijah breathes, meeting us when we descend the stage. "Nimra, that was *amazing*. It was incredible. It was—" She can't think of another synonym. Being that she's our toughest critic, I'd say it's a good sign.

"We did it!" Bilal exclaims, pumping the air and jumping up and down. "Did you guys see that?"

"Yeah, Bilal. We were kinda there," says Matthew. He's grinning from ear to ear.

Waleed's face is pink with joy. "I've never felt a rush like that in my entire life. They loved us. Really loved us."

"That last part, though," Bilal continues to gush, celebrating in his own little world. "That *beat*. And our duet. All hail Princess Nimra!"

Our families swarm us. Baba envelops me in his arms, spinning me around in a circle. His eyes are red from crying. "I knew you were good, but that was unreal. You made us so proud." Mama kisses me all over my face. Sister Sadia, Nano, Nana, and the rest of my family take turns praising us.

Waleed's parents and brother pat him on the back. His dad nods his approval. "I'm impressed, son. You make a fine musician. Maybe we should sign you up for advanced classes." Waleed wears a look of elation while my heart bursts with joy for him.

Bilal and Khadijah's parents hug them. Matthew's mom hands him baby Zoya. He introduces me to her. She grabs my finger, making gleeful noises. The adults take the opportunity to greet and congratulate one another.

"Mash Allah," says Khadijah's mom. "Our children are so talented."

"Yes, they are," agrees Matthew's dad.

"Okay, folks." The emcee returns to the stage, waving a piece of paper in his hands. "The judges have reached a decision. After thoughtful consideration, the winner of the talent show iiiisssssss—BARAKAH BEATS! Congratulations! Free Six Flags tickets are yours!"

The five of us grab hold of one another and bounce and scream. Our families rejoice even louder this time.

"So, what's next for Barakah Beats?" asks Matthew's mom. "After tonight, your fan base is going to explode."

Waleed shrugs, meeting my eyes. "I don't know. But it sure will never be the same again."

He's right and also not. Middle school will always be the fifth circle of hell. But that doesn't mean I have to go through it alone. In the end, even though I've chosen not to participate in the music directly, I'm still getting from my new friends so much of what I loved about singing with them: the people, the community, the teamwork. And thanks to the people who believed in me, I'm more confident in pursuing what really makes my heart sing: art.

It took a long time, but I've finally opened my eyes to the truth. As long as there are those who love us for who we are, we don't have to be the rough sketch version of ourselves.

We can be the final product.

28

"Thirteen minutes," Khadijah announces.

I stuff the rest of my pizza bites in my mouth while she hurriedly cleans up our scraps. This is our A-day lunch routine now. We spend exactly seventeen minutes eating and talking in the cafeteria. When there's exactly thirteen minutes left of lunch, we get up to go to the bathroom. It's just enough time to make wudu and read Zuhr before the block ends. It took us a few tries to nail down because we had to work out a deal with Barakah Beats about how to share the space.

We walk past Jenna's table, and just like the last two weeks, she won't look at me. We haven't talked or walked to school together since that day I told her off. I miss her sometimes, but then I look at Khadijah and that feeling disappears.

Julie's the only one at the table who meets my eyes and smiles. We've been hanging out more in PE when Jenna's off being Jenna. When Julie's not saving my nose from being broken, she's usually telling me about her mom's art decor business. I wouldn't call her my friend, but I think we're getting there. Out of everything that has happened since school started, that surprises me the most.

Exactly three minutes later (we count), Khadijah and I are done making wudu and stand to pray in the small space across from the main band room. Seven more minutes later, we're both done and roll up our prayer mats. Then we take our stuff and walk to the other room.

Waleed, Matthew, and Bilal look up at our arrival.

"Better?" Bilal asks, grinning.

"Didn't hear a peep." Khadijah slow claps. "Good job. I know how hard it must be for you guys to stay quiet for seven whole minutes while we pray."

"Thank Waleed's writer's block," says Matthew. He

has one foot relaxed on the chair in front of him. His guitar is in its case for once. "We've been stuck on this piece for a while."

Waleed shrugs, which is a big deal since it's him we're talking about. The ADAMS show changed everything for Barakah Beats. They're known outside school now, too, especially in our Muslim community. Waleed's learned to take things easier with the band since his dad finally started supporting him. Everyone knows at this point I'm not part of Barakah Beats anymore, but I still call myself their number one fan.

Bilal crosses his hands behind his head and sighs dramatically. "If only someone extremely talented could help us fix this song." He bats his eyelashes at me.

"Leave her alone, Bilal," Matthew chides.

"If you were cute, maybe that eye thing would work," says Khadijah.

I laugh. These last three minutes of A-day lunch are the only time at school when the five of us are together. I can tell by everyone's face that they miss the old days. They miss me being part of the band. Sometimes it's hard not to follow Waleed here after algebra. The fight between my heart and mind is real. My new friends are so supportive, though. They don't judge me for how I choose to practice Islam.

"Who's excited for Six Flags this weekend?" Waleed asks. All our families planned a big trip to the amusement park. We're even renting a party bus.

Khadijah, Matthew, and I raise our hands. "Yeah!"

Bilal slouches in his chair, mumbling something about hating rides.

"He's a scaredy-cat," Khadijah tells us. "Won't even go on the kiddie rides."

"Aw. Don't worry." Waleed rubs Bilal's shoulder, teasing. "Bring an extra stroller and Zoya will keep you company."

We all snicker at Bilal's dirty look. "You know what? I don't care. Zoya and I are going to start our own club and none of you are invited to our crib."

"Pretty sure my baby sister's going to be out of the crib before you," Matthew says.

"You know that's not what I meant!" Bilal argues as Khadijah bends over laughing.

While they bicker, I go over to sit next to Waleed. I look at the open notebook on his knees, at the scribbles and crossed-out lyrics. He has graphite all over his fingers like I do when I'm sketching. Most of the pictures I post are drawn by hand. My three hundred followers prefer those over the digitally colored ones, too. More people have been reposting my work with credits lately and it's so cool to see.

"Where are you stuck?" I ask.

Waleed shakes his head, covering the page with his hand. "It's okay, Nimra. Bilal was joking. You don't have to help. I'll figure it out."

"Waleed," I say, "just 'cause I'm not singing with you guys anymore doesn't mean you can't ask for my opinion."

Waleed glances at me, surprised. "Really? I didn't want to put you on the spot."

"Just send me a picture of what you have. I'll try to look at it next block."

"Thanks, Nimra. Hey, I've been meaning to ask you . . ." Waleed taps his pencil against his knee. "We're making an album for the first time—just putting all our songs in one place with some new ones—and I was hoping maybe you could draw a cover for us? Only if you want," he adds quickly. "I understand if you don't."

My eyes practically pop out of my head. "Are you serious? Of course I want to! When do you need it by? I can start on it right away. In fact, I'll get a couple of rough sketches to you by next A day and we can all vote—"

"Slow down, slow down. There's no hurry. We've got plenty of time."

I smile, because he's right. We've got all the time in the world.

What matters is that we make every beat count.

AUTHOR'S NOTE

Music in Islam is a hotly contested debate in the ummah. Nimra and her family's views on music stem from my own personal experiences and preferences for how I engage with my faith. I in no way expect other Muslims to follow this example, nor do I mean any disrespect to those whose views are the opposite. I tried my best to write and edit with compassion and I'm truly sorry if anything in the text offends. Religion and connection to God are deeply personal matters. Regardless of what is and is not allowed in Islam, Muslims are not a monolith. We practice in different ways, the ways that feel right to us. Nimra and her family's opinions are just one of a multifaceted, diverse, and beautiful global community. Let us respect one another's boundaries without having to sacrifice our own imans. And just as is mentioned in the book, in the end, no one but Allah (SWT) has the right to judge us.

ACKNOWLEDGMENTS

When I first started writing *Barakah Beats* in November of 2018, I knew deep down that it was the book that would make me a published author. Still, I was terrified that no one would connect or want to give Nimra's story a chance—that she would be perceived as "too Muslim" or her dedication and love for her Islamic faith "not believable" for a young third-generation American girl. But someone did. More people than I could have ever imagined gave Nimra, Waleed, Matthew, Bilal, and Khadijah their chance in the spotlight, and I would like to thank them for their support.

First and foremost, my literary agent, Lauren Spieller. Lauren, thank you for your patience, for taking the time to ask questions, and for understanding the story I wanted to tell. My heart still swells with joy whenever I think about how you just *got* it. You gave Nimra the wings she needed to fly. I couldn't have asked for a better advocate for my books. You are an answer to my prayers.

To my editor, Emily Seife. When you gave me your magical editorial feedback on our first phone call, I knew this book was meant to be in your capable hands. Thank you for guiding me and for helping to usher Nimra's story into the world. I'm so lucky to have the chance to work with you. My warmest gratitude to everyone else in the Scholastic family who played a role in bringing *Barakah Beats* to life, especially Mary Kate Garmire, Janell Harris, Taylan Salvati, and Rachel Feld.

To my book cover artist, Javeria M. Talha, and designer Yaffa Jaskoll. Thank you for literally reaching into my brain and rendering Nimra and the crew better than I could've ever imagined! It means so much to me that kids will be able to look at this cover and see themselves front and center.

To Anjana Radhakrishnan, for being the first person to read *Barakah Beats*'s first draft and being so sure that it would be available on shelves one day. Many thanks to Kit Rosewater for being an early reader and generously giving me such wonderful notes.

To Laura Weymouth, for your endless love and support and for being my first friend in the writing community. And thank you, S. K. Ali, for your books, for being the first Muslim writer that I connected with, and for allowing me to share my hopes and fears with you.

Thank you, Lauren Blackwood, for always being just a text message away. You never fail to put a smile on my face, and I'm so glad we got to ride the debut train together. Also, thank you to Fahduma Majid for always cheering me on, and to Marium Mehdi for taking my author photos!

Thank you to all of my lovely cousins and siblings who made the celebration of my first book deal so memorable. I love you all so much. Shout-out goes to my sister, Nawal, for always putting up with my flailing and not understanding a word of publishing jargon, but always being excited for me anyway.

To my parents, for immigrating to this country and giving me and my siblings the opportunities they never had. You survived so that we could thrive.

To my husband, Usman, my biggest champion. Thank you for all the late-night pep talks in the car. Thank you for never letting me quit my dreams, for believing in them even more than I did. Thank you for standing by my side and doing life with all its ups and downs with me and for being the most amazing baba to our daughter.

I wrote this book for the Muslim kids who rarely get the chance to see themselves portrayed positively in stories. I hope Nimra's journey to self-acceptance brings you hope and the courage to live your own lives without worrying about what other people will think. Your relationship with your deen is your own. Embrace it with your whole hearts. Only when I embraced mine did Nimra's story pour out of me.

And lastly, thank you, Allah (SWT). For all the times You were the only one who listened, who saw my tears. You promise, "Take one step towards me, I will take ten steps towards you. Walk towards me, I will run towards you." But I took one step towards You, and You sprinted to meet me the rest of the way. None of this would have been possible without You.

Read on for a sneak peek at
Bhai for Now by Maleeha Siddiqui!

1

SHAHEER

Shaheer threw an armload of clothes onto the bed of his fourth bedroom in four years and kicked the empty box out into the hallway. He couldn't stand the smell of cardboard. Maybe if his life wasn't like a train that barely stopped long enough to let people on and off, he wouldn't hate it as much. At least he wouldn't be around it all the freakin' time.

"Ah, someone finally decided to unpack," Dad said, appearing in the doorway with a mug of chai.

"Look who's talking. You live out of a suitcase," Shaheer deadpanned.

"Not anymore. I hung my clothes up," Dad said proudly. "On real hangers."

Shaheer rolled his eyes. He didn't see the point in

setting up his room, and it wasn't like he had a lot of stuff anyway. None of them did. Their next destination was always on the horizon. It was inevitable, like getting half a cheese slice on a McDonald's fish filet sandwich. Their time in every city ended with them saying goodbye, and this spot in Northern Virginia would be next. Shaheer knew they were only going to be there temporarily, no matter what lies Dad fed him about this being "it." As if. Shaheer might believe it if he, Dad, and Dada slept on real beds instead of mattresses, put up curtains for once, and didn't eat off disposable plates all the time.

Dad sipped his chai and peered at Shaheer over the mug's rim. "You excited for school tomorrow?"

Shaheer gave Dad a *What do you think?* look. After years of hopping around from school to school, he'd learned it was easier to hold back and roll with the punches. He almost forgot what it was like to put his feelings into words. Shaheer let his silence do all the talking now.

"Do me a favor, sport?" Dad said. "Please try to get involved this time. Make friends. Join a club. Go to the masjid."

The *masjid?* When was the last time Shaheer had set foot in one? Did this have something to do with how he'd thrown a fit the whole month of Ramadan? Shaheer technically should have fasted more than the seven days his dad and grandfather had managed to crank out of him. But it wasn't like Dad prayed five times a day or anything. In fact, Shaheer was pretty sure he didn't even attend Friday prayers regularly. If Dad wanted him to do those things, then *he* should try doing them himself first.

Instead, Dad spent all his energy chasing the next shiny hospital job like it was a pot of gold at the end of a rainbow. Shaheer had no clue what Dad got out of it.

"What do you say?" Dad asked, continuing the one-way conversation. Shaheer brushed past him to the kitchen of the three-bedroom apartment.

"Sure. Whatever," said Shaheer. He pretended to search for a snack, but the only thing he could find was leftover salad that came with the gyros they'd had for lunch. It was all soggy, but Dada refused to throw food away unless it'd gone beyond bad. Well, someone had to eat it, and Shaheer didn't feel like going back to the room that would never be *his*, or give Dad the chance to keep talking to him. He took up the plate of salad, grabbed a disposable fork, and flopped down on Dada's favorite armchair in the living room near where his grandfather was making dua.

Shaheer chewed on a limp piece of lettuce as he waited for his grandfather to finish praying. When Dada finally looked up from his splayed hands, Shaheer asked him, "What do you ask so hard for?" Dada took so long making dua that sometimes Shaheer had to poke him to make sure he was still alive.

"Oh, you know," he said wistfully. Dada sounded younger than sixty-four. He was like a sturdy, uncracked beam that could still hold up the whole house. "Jannah for your dadi. Health. A full head of hair. Hey, we're supposed to believe in miracles!" he exclaimed when Shaheer smirked. "We'll see who gets the last laugh when, God willing, you get to my age."

Shaheer smoothed back his hair fondly. It had grown out longer than it'd ever been and started curling at the nape of his neck and falling into his eyes. His hair was the only thing about his appearance he liked, and the thought of it falling out made him feel faint.

"Way to scare him, Abba," Dad piped up. He was sitting with his legs crossed against the wall dividing the kitchen from the living room. That wall, Shaheer thought, was a waste of space. It could be taken out and replaced with an island so that the place looked more open. This apartment was nicer than some of the others they'd lived in, but it didn't get the Property Brothers' seal of approval.

Shaheer had had no clue what "open concept" or "clean lines" meant until a few years ago when they were stuck inside the house for months during a global pandemic. At one point, Dad stayed at the hospital for a whole month to care for patients in the ER and to avoid bringing the virus home, especially since Dada was high risk. That was when Dada morphed into a devout HGTV watcher to distract himself from worrying about Dad. Shaheer had never been so happy to see Dad as the day when he finally came home. That was back when the two of them were still tight.

Shaheer didn't get Dada's interior design obsession at first, but when he started joining him out of sheer boredom, he suddenly started noticing how subtle transformations lit up people's faces. How the way a house changed to suit a particular family's needs suddenly made it a *home*. Shaheer thought it was cool that the twins on *Property Brothers* worked together. He didn't have siblings or a Forever Home. Shaheer might never have either of those things at this rate, so he had to settle for being happy for others who did.

"What are you eating?" Dada asked, peering at Shaheer's plate.

"The day's special," said Shaheer, thrusting a piece of tomato into his mouth.

"Why didn't you tell me you were hungry?" Dad said. "I would've ordered us pizza."

"No, no. We've eaten out too much these last few days. It's time I made us a real dinner," Dada said. "Jawad, did you unbox the masala jars? You did the groceries yesterday, right? Great. Here, give me this." Dada took the sad-looking salad out of Shaheer's hands. "I'll finish it. How about I make you anda salan?"

Shaheer sat up. Anda salan was egg curry with cut-up potatoes tossed in. It was the most basic of basic Pakistani dishes, and one of the few things Dada knew how to cook. Shaheer, who rarely got homemade meals, thought it was delicious. And he liked knowing that Dada had gotten the recipe from Shaheer's mom years ago.

Shaheer had never met his mom. His parents had divorced when he was a baby. He didn't know much besides her name because the one time he'd been curious about her, Dad shut him down. Hard. Made it clear the topic was off-limits. He'd been happier to answer Shaheer's burning questions about puberty when he was ten.

Shaheer had never even seen a picture of his mom. When he thought about it, it wasn't normal. No pictures of someone his dad had supposedly loved enough to marry and have a kid with?

As Dada headed toward the kitchen, Shaheer scampered to retrieve their one giant pot in the lower kitchen cabinet and put it on the stove himself before Dada could. Dada had back problems and wasn't allowed to bend over a lot. Shaheer always made sure Dada wasn't doing anything that could get himself hurt, even though it made Dada grumble about not being *that* old. Like now. He muttered to himself as he boiled eggs with his reading glasses sitting atop his head.

"Really, Abba. I could've had something delivered. You don't have to stand for so long," Dad said.

"Bah," Dada said, waving him off. "Not that old yet. My feet are fine. So are yours, Dr. Atique. Put 'em to good use and add some rice to the cooker. Shaheer, get me a tomato and one potato, please. Now, what were you two talking about earlier? Allah forgive me, I was listening while reading namaz."

"Oh, I was telling Shaheer that he should do some kind of activity. Remember how many extracurriculars I used to do in school?" Dad said, measuring out a cup of rice.

"That's 'cuz you were a show-off," Dada said in Urdu. Shaheer pressed his lips together to keep from grinning.

"But don't you think it's true?" Dad asked. "It'd be better than coming straight home every day." Dad was a total wanderer. When he wasn't working, he loved to get out of the house and explore new places or try new things. Shaheer stopped joining Dad two moves ago out of defiance. What was the point in getting to know a place you'd just leave behind?

"He lives like this because you refuse to give the boy a chance to make a life somewhere." Leave it to Dada to not beat around the bush.

"What about a sport?" Dad said like he hadn't heard him. "Or volunteer work."

"Shaheer's not you, Jawad," Dada said gently. "Let him decide for himself."

Dad's eyebrows pinched in Dada's direction, his hand going still over the rice cooker. "What's that supposed to mean? I'm not allowed to give my own son advice?"

"Yes, I'm well aware he's *your* son, thanks," said Dada.

Shaheer sighed, watching Dada slice the tomato with a little too much force. Honestly, what was their deal? Dad and Dada were almost always fine. Then at random times certain comments unleashed some old feud and they never clued Shaheer in. Shaheer was used to it, and it was usually the perfect distraction for him when he wanted to be alone, but the bad mojo lingered in the air for too long afterward.

Dad muttered something about Dada never taking his side and moved to the sink to soak the rice.

"He's always been restless," Dada whispered to Shaheer. "Hard for him to stay in one place for too long. You should say something to him about it, too, you know. He never listens to me, not since he was a kid. Not even when—" Dada stopped short and got this faraway look in his eyes. It happened sometimes, Dada's mood shifting out of the blue, and Shaheer never understood why. There was no way Dad thought Shaheer liked all the moving around. If he couldn't see something so obvious, then what was the point in *telling* him?

"Anyway," Dada continued as he cut the potato into squares. "It's not a bad idea. Maybe a recreational activity is what you need." Shaheer's forehead crinkled. "Not saying you have to, but give it some thought. In shaa Allah, you won't have to live like this forever."

Shaheer's mind buzzed. He imagined what it would be like to make friends he wouldn't have to leave behind.

To not be afraid of getting attached to a place because it always ended up in the rearview mirror as they drove away again. The longing squeezed his heart, but Shaheer knew his options: face disappointment or don't bother to care.

Shaheer didn't bother. He was over it.